TO THE
OF THE OCEAN

Also in this trilogy:

Book 1: Troubled Waters
Book 3: Bright Horizon

TO THE EDGE
OF THE OCEAN

ROSEMARY HAYES

Hodder
Children's
Books

a division of Hodder Headline Limited

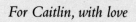

For Caitlin, with love

1

London, June 1861

Amos sat at his bench, jabbing at a strip of leather. He knew what he should be doing; he'd been well taught. Too well taught. He was bored with the whole business.

He should be making regular holes in the stirrup leathers to attach to the saddle that Uncle Edward had just put in front of him. It was a special saddle – for Lord Fanshaw's best hunter – and as he glanced at it he could see how well it was finished, the hand-tooling and stitching expertly done and the leather soft and pliable.

He sighed and looked out of the small, dirty window. It was a fine summer's day and folk in the street outside were strolling by in the heat. On the corner there was a cart and beside it a sherbert seller, yelling for custom.

Amos gave the saddle a vicious poke. 'Fanshaw! Damn toff!' he muttered. But he spoke very quietly, so no one could hear. Everyone else who worked in Uncle Edward's harness-making business was in awe of

Lord Fanshaw, but Amos scowled at the very mention of his name.

He couldn't forget that his mother, Sarah, had once been a lowly under maid in Fanshaw's grand house in Cavendish Square. And Aunt Abbie – Uncle Edward's wife – she'd been a maid there, too, before they'd seen how handy she was with her needle and made a dressmaker out of her. And then there was all the mystery about his father, Jim, and the house in Cavendish Square. His mother and his uncle and aunt never spoke about Jim, but sometimes Amos overheard snatches of whispered conversation: '. . . really good of his lordship to forgive and forget . . . where would we be if he'd told all his friends about Jim? . . . we'd not have any of the carriage trade that we have today.'

The carriage trade. That meant the smart turnouts and special orders for hunting saddles, and sometimes even racing saddles too. This sort of trade brought in good money; much better than mending the old harnesses for the tradesmen with their horses and carts.

Amos scratched a deep score into the wooden bench and looked at it with satisfaction. He was sick of the smell of leather, sick of cutting and stitching and stuffing and making holes and fixing buckles. He felt restless and he found himself thinking more and more about his dead father.

Amos had been six when Jim left, but he could remember him still. He remembered the laughter, the hugs and the teasing. He chose to forget the shouting and the drinking and how he and his mother and brother were often cold and hungry.

He'd always been curious about Jim, but now that he was grown-up it nagged away at him; now he really wanted to know. What had Jim *done*? Why had he run away and left them?

He couldn't get anything out of Sarah. She would just sigh quietly. 'You *know* what 'appened, Amos. You know that your father drowned at sea.'

'But before then, Mam? What 'appened before then?'

'It's all in the past, Amos,' was all that Sarah would say. And, if he pressed her, she'd just get angry. 'Leave it be, will you, Amos? No point dragging all that up now. It's all over, thank the Lord. And thanks to Abbie and Edward, you and me and your brother have a good place to live and decent work to do. You should go down on your knees, boy, and be thankful for what you have.'

Thankful! How many times a day did he have to be thankful?

Amos hated being thankful. When he delivered orders to the grand houses up west, he had to be thankful. He had to doff his cap and bow and scrape to Lord Fanshaw and all the other toffs who gave Uncle Edward business. And he was never to forget to be thankful to Edward and Abbie, too, for giving him a job and a home.

Amos looked up and caught the eye of his twin brother, Seth, who was busy cutting a piece of leather.

His cousin, James – Edward's son – was beside Seth. He was holding the leather steady. Seth grinned at Amos and winked.

Although they were twins, there could be no more different people than Amos and Seth. Amos was dark, with brooding good looks, while Seth was fair and open-faced. Everyone loved Seth, with his easy ways, his good humour and his charm. Even Amos loved him, though deep down he was jealous of him too. Sarah had always favoured Seth and it was easy to see why. Right from the start, Seth had been no trouble, but Amos had always been difficult, bad-tempered and moody.

Now they were both young men of eighteen. Seth seemed contented with life but Amos was fed up with working for his uncle. A few days ago, he'd said this to Sarah and she'd been more angry than he'd seen her for years.

' 'Ow can you be so ungrateful, Amos? Your Aunt Abbie and Uncle Edward saw to it that you and Seth went to school and learned your letters with your cousins, and now they've seen to it that you're learning a decent trade. You don't know 'ow lucky you are!'

'*Lucky*!' said Amos. '*Lucky*! when I'm always 'aving to show how grateful I am! Licking everyone's boots, pulling my forelock. "Yessir, this, yessir that. Thank you sir. Much obliged sir. Oh and *thank you* Uncle Edward, *thank you* Aunt Abbie." I'm sick of it I tell you. I want to get away, see a bit more life, mother. I've never known

anything else! I want to get out of this place. I want—'
But Amos had suddenly stopped. Sarah was still and her
back was rigid. He could sense her mounting anger and
it frightened him. Then she'd turned on him, red-faced
and furious.

'My God, Amos, there's a big helping of your father in
you. Always wanting what you can't 'ave. Never content.
You don't know the 'alf of it, boy.'

'*What* don't I know, Mam?' Amos yelled. 'Why won't
you *tell* me?'

Sarah looked him straight in the eye. 'I've told you
before and I'll tell you again, Amos, I'm not going to go
raking up the past. But just remember this, son. Because
of your father and his ways, there was a time when I was
forced to live on the streets!'

Amos stared at her, lost for words. Sarah looked at his
shocked face.

'Oh yes, Amos,' she said, quietly. 'I've known what it's
like to be starving and cold and stinking and wretched,
just trying to earn enough to keep you two boys alive.
I've been in places and seen things that I pray that
you and Seth will never see, so don't let me ever
'ear you talk this way again. You will learn to be a
good harness-maker and you'll help your uncle all you
can, do you understand?'

Since that conversation, Amos had said no more about
getting away. But he hadn't stopped thinking about it.

He dragged his mind back to the present and drew

the stirrup leathers towards him, but he continued to wonder about his mother's words.

Sarah was plump and pretty. Most days she worked at Aunt Abbie's dress shop – serving the customers, taking the money and, when Abbie wasn't there, keeping a firm eye on the three girls Abbie was training up to be dressmakers. Abbie's daughter, Victoria, was one of them and it was plain to see that she had the same flair as her mother.

Amos couldn't imagine his neat, well turned-out mother ever being in the state she described – filthy and starving.

What had happened in the past? What had his father done?

Uncle Edward's voice broke into his thoughts. 'Hurry up, Amos, that saddle has to be delivered today, not next week!'

Amos picked up the awl and the measuring tape, and started piercing the holes at regular intervals down the leather. And every time he pierced a hole, he thought: 'But I want more than this. I don't want to be doing this day in, day out. I don't want to be a harness-maker all my life.'

Uncle Edward kept him busy for the rest of the day delivering finished saddles and bridles and fetching harnesses to repair. In the evening he, Seth and James helped Uncle Edward close up the shop and then Seth and Amos started to go home to Sarah. But after they'd walked a little way, Amos stopped.

'Come on, Amos,' said Seth. 'Hurry up. I'm starving. Let's go home and eat.'

Starving! The word, so carelessly said, meant something different now.

Amos shook his head. 'I'm going for a walk,' he said gruffly.

Seth was used to his twin's changes of mood. 'Then I'll come along with you,' he said cheerfully.

Amos shrugged and set off down towards the river. Seth kept up a constant chatter about the customers they'd seen that day, the problems with this saddle or that, the people and things they passed.

Amos wasn't listening.

'Seth?' he said at last, stopping and looking at his brother.

'Yes?'

'Do you want to stay being a harnessmaker all your life? Don't you want to do sommat else?'

'Sommat else?'

'Make your way in the world. Get away from 'ere.'

Seth frowned and shook his head. 'But what would I do? Why would I want to leave?'

Amos smiled and put his arm round Seth's shoulders.

'No, you're right, Seth. You're happy being 'ere. You're content. Take no notice of me.'

They walked on in silence until they came to the

7

banks of the Thames, where they stopped and looked out over the wide grey river, noisy with boats and screaming gulls.

'Our grandad was a Thames waterman,' said Amos, suddenly.

'What, Mam's dad? No 'e wasn't, he was—'

'No,' said Amos, impatiently, 'the other grandad.'

'Our father's dad?'

Amos nodded.

'How d'you know that?'

'I've bin thinking about father alot.'

He bent down and picked up a stone and hurled it into the river, then watched as it hit the water and the ripples spread out, further and further. He sighed.

'I asked Aunt Abbie. She told me about Grandfather. She said it was the Thames with its cold and damp that killed 'im.'

Seth's eyes widened. 'Did you ask her about father, too?'

Amos nodded. 'I asked. But they won't say nothing. Ma goes silent and angry. Aunt Abbie just looks sad.'

'Well, he was her brother. Mebbe she's ashamed of 'im, ashamed of whatever 'e did.'

Amos nodded. 'She never says aught bad about him though – not like Mam.'

Seth was curious. 'What *does* she say, then?'

Amos shrugged. 'Just that life gave him a rotten deal.'

'Nothing else?'

'Not much. She told me that he was a bright lad, but then things changed and he went to the bad.'

'No point dwelling on it then,' said Seth.

Amos frowned. He was still staring out over the water. 'I reckon there's a lot of Grandfather in me, Seth.'

'What d'you mean?'

'Oh, I dunno. the water. I love the water – and boats. Where they've bin, where they're going.'

Seth grinned. 'You've never bin on a boat in yer life!'

'Aye, but I'd like to,' muttered Amos. 'I'd like to see new places. Visit foreign lands.'

'What, and leave us all behind?' Seth was still grinning.

Amos looked at him, his sullen face suddenly animated. 'You could come, too, Seth. We could go together.'

'Don't be soft. I 'ate the water – and anyways, I'm a harness-maker, not a sailor. I'd most likely drown like our father.'

Amos turned and looked at his brother. 'Aunt Abbie did tell me one thing about Father,' he said slowly.

'What was that?'

'She said, when they were young, he'd sometimes go out on the water with Grandfather.' Amos hesitated. He kicked at a pile of rotting vegetation which lay at his feet. 'She said he could swim like a little fish.'

Seth laughed. 'Well, that's more than we can. If anyone tipped us in the river, we'd sink like stones.' Seth stretched and yawned. 'Come on, Amos. Let's go home.'

Amos shook his head. 'I'm not 'ungry. Tell Mam I'll be back later.'

'She won't like it,' said Seth, mildly.

Amos looked angry. 'I'm a man now – so are you. We're not mewling babes tied to 'er apron strings.'

Seth quickly changed the subject. 'Where are you going?'

'I'll stay 'ere for a bit. I like it 'ere.'

Seth shrugged, clapped his brother on the back and turned on his heel.

Amos watched him stride away. When Seth reached the corner of the street, he looked back and waved. Amos raised his hand and then, when Seth was out of sight, he walked upstream in the direction of the docks.

Bedford, December, present day

I've just looked at the last entry in this notebook. It was more than a year ago.

Things had just turned the corner for us then. That creep Keith, who was living with Mum, had left and gone to another job up north and – after months of worry – we'd found Matt. Found him safe and well.

Matt had changed though; of course he'd changed. He was seventeen, nearly eighteen, when he got in touch. He wasn't the brother I'd known. He'd had to grow up fast, living in the hostel, coping on his own. But he'd been lucky. He'd had some good support and some great teachers at the school he went to in London. They'd encouraged him with his music and he and his new band had made a CD. They'd called the band Jacob's Footstool. One day, out of the blue, he'd sent me their CD – and there was an email address for the band on it. That's how we got back in touch.

We still don't see much of him. I don't blame him. He likes being in London and he had a lot of bad memories from here – Keith, for one, and then being accused of stealing stuff from our school. But he'd put it all behind him, and Mum and me thought he was doing really well. Whenever we saw him he was funny and cool. I was really proud of him, and so was Mum.

It's been a time of change for us all. Me and Mum have moved to a new house, Mum's got a job and some new friends, and Katie (my best friend) and me both have boyfriends. Well, Katie has and I have this guy Tom who fancies me, but I don't really fancy him, to be honest.

But, on the whole, things are going really well for all of us. So yesterday was a real shock.

I don't know what to do, whether I should tell Mum or not. But I must get it clear in my head. So I'm writing it down. It's funny; I only seem to write stuff in this book when I'm worried.

Yesterday, Saturday, I decided to go shopping for Christmas presents in London. Usually, when I go to London, I go with Katie. But Katie's so wrapped up in lover-boy that she didn't want to come, so I went on my own. Mum was a bit off about it, but, as I pointed out to her, I'm nearly sixteen, I know my way about the underground and, anyway, I was only going to

11

Oxford Street. So she agreed, shouting after me as I got on the train, 'Have you got your mobile?'. I pretended I'd left it behind, just to see her panic for a moment, then I waved it at her and grinned. Honestly, mothers! She knows I don't go anywhere without it.

Anyway, I surprised myself and managed to buy all the things on my list really quickly, and it was still only early afternoon. I didn't want to go home so I decided to go and call in on Matt to surprise him.

Matt lives in a tiny flat near Euston Station, so it wasn't far to go. When I got to the flat, I rang the bell. It took ages for a voice to come through the intercom.

But when the voice did come through, it wasn't Matt. And it wasn't the lad he shares with, either. I suddenly felt uneasy. 'It's Becky,' I said. 'Matt's sister.' Then there was a long pause, so I said, 'Can I come up?'

'No,' said the voice. Then, after a bit. 'Matt doesn't live here any more.'

And then the intercom went dead.

I stood there for ages on the steps. It was really odd. Matt hadn't said anything about moving. But maybe he wouldn't have?

All the way home I had this awful feeling in my stomach. The feeling I'd had when he was missing.

He wouldn't disappear again, would he?

I keep telling myself that he's just moved flats — simple as that. He'll be in touch. No need to make a big deal out of it. He'd hate us to fuss.

But when I got home, it didn't feel right, somehow.

I couldn't sleep last night. I kept telling myself that it was different now. We knew how to reach him. He'd be in touch soon.

But I couldn't shift that feeling of dread.

In the middle of the night, I got up and looked at the presents I'd bought. I'd got a really great compilation CD for Matt. One I know he wants.

I wonder if he'll come for Christmas?

I'll try and get in touch again tomorrow. He doesn't have a mobile; I guess he doesn't like people knowing where he is every minute of the day. But I can send a message to the band's email address.

London, June 1861

At last Amos left the docks and turned for home. He'd walked all the way to Shadwell and it was a long way back, but he was restless and full of energy. He hardly noticed the distance.

He didn't go straight home to Sarah and Seth. Instead, he walked past their lodgings and went towards the house where Uncle Edward and Aunt Abbie lived. It was only a few doors down from the shop where he worked. He paused there first and stared into the barred window. Then he walked round the back to the stable where the two horses were kept. For a few minutes he stood, stroking their noses, whispering to them, and then he took a deep breath and strode the few paces back to Edward and Abbie's place.

When he banged on the door, Edward opened it. If Edward was surprised, he didn't show it.

'Come in lad, sit down.'

But Amos didn't sit down. He stayed standing and fiddled nervously with his braces.

'Is Aunt Abbie 'ere?' he asked.

Edward did look surprised then. 'Yes, she's out the back, Amos, clearing away our meal.'

'I'd like to speak to her.'

Edward nodded and Amos walked past him and through into the little kitchen at the back. He found Abbie drying pans with a clout. Her back was to him and she was humming. He stood silently, watching her until she turned round. She jumped when she saw him.

'Oh Amos, how you startled me!' she said.

'Beg pardon,' he mumbled.

Abbie dried her hands and looked at him. He so often reminded her of her dead brother, Jim, and she could read his expression as well as she had read Jim's in the past. He was a difficult boy – always had been – and troubled and restless, like his father came to be.

'What is it, Amos?'

Amos picked up a wooden spoon and turned it over and over in his hands.

'I want to know about my father,' he said, without looking up.

Abbie sat down on one of the kitchen chairs. She put her hands in her lap.

'It's all in the past, Amos,' she said gently. 'No point dwelling on it.'

Amos banged his fist against the wall in fury.

'That's what you *all* say! Whenever I ask about him.'

'But Amos—!'

'Don't I have a right to know?' he shouted.

Uncle Edward came in. 'What's this, Amos?' he said angrily. 'I won't 'ave you raising your voice to your aunt!'

Abbie looked up. 'It's all right, Edward. Leave us be.'

Edward frowned but then he caught Abbie's almost imperceptible nod of dismissal. He hesitated, then walked slowly back to the front room.

'Sit down, Amos,' said Abbie, pointing at the other chair.

Suddenly, Amos felt tears coming to his eyes. Furious, he brushed them aside and sat down.

'I just want to know,' he said hoarsely.

Abbie said nothing.

'And Mam won't tell me anything.'

'No,' said Abbie. 'Well, your Mam was poorly treated by 'im, Amos. She's very bitter and who can blame 'er?'

'Please tell me, Aunt Abbie. Just tell me what 'e did. Why 'e was that bad?'

15

Abbie sighed. 'You're right, Amos. You and Seth are grown men now. No point in keeping it from you, if you really want to know.'

'I do. 'Owever bad it is.'

Abbie nodded slowly. She dried her hands carefully on the clout before she spoke.

'I don't know where to start, Amos,' she said.

'From when you were children together?'

Abbie smiled. ' 'E was a fine lad, your father, Amos. We were that poor, our family. My mam took in sewing – mending and darning – and my pa was a Thames waterman like I told you.' Absently, she smoothed the clout and folded it. 'Me and Jim worked the Whitechapel market, 'elping out, running errands and that. It were 'ard work, I can tell you, but we were 'appy.'

'So – what 'appened?'

'It's a long story, Amos, but I'll give you the bare bones. Jim was a cheeky lad, but not a bad one. But he cheeked someone once too often and he paid an 'eavy price.' She coughed, then went on. ' 'E was accused of stealing a gentleman's watch, Amos. 'E never did it, mind, but 'e were convicted and sent off to a place called Point Puer – a prison for boys – in the colonies, in Van Dieman's Land.'

Amos frowned. He'd only vaguely heard of Van Dieman's Land.

'It were a harsh place for a young lad, Amos, and

it changed your father for ever. Six long years he was there, rotting and suffering for a crime 'e never even committed.'

'So, when he came back . . . ?'

'When 'e came back he was that bitter. He turned to crime, then. Said it was all 'e knew 'ow to do.'

'Did 'e take stuff from Lord Fanshaw?' said Amos suddenly.

Abbie started and then reddened. 'Yes, he did,' she said quietly. 'He took jewellery and trinkets and . . . and a snuff box.'

'An' did he run away to sea, or what?'

Abbie swallowed. 'The police were on to 'im, Amos. 'E went to a sailor 'e knew who got 'im a working passage back to Australia.'

'An' then 'e drowned?'

She nodded. 'Yes, Amos. Months later, 'is sailor friend came to see us and told us that they'd been shipwrecked and only a few had escaped.'

'But my father wasn't one of them?'

'No, Amos, Jim wasn't one of them.'

Amos was quiet for a bit, then he said shakily. 'So 'e just upped and left with no word to Mam?'

Abbie bit her lip. 'No, he never told Sarah, but . . . but he told me.'

'Why? Why didn't he tell Mam?'

Abbie chose her words carefully. 'I think he thought, if she knew, the police would get it out of 'er.'

She looked into his face; so like his father, with the dark good looks.

'Don't think ill of him, Amos. It were life that played him a bad 'and.'

'But . . . to leave with no thought of Mam . . . or us!'

' 'E did spare you a thought, Amos,' said Abbie quietly.

' 'Ow d'you mean?'

Abbie stood up. 'You know this much, you might as well know the rest. Come with me.' Abbie took a key from a bunch round her waist and Amos followed her into the other room. She went over to her desk and unlocked it.

Edward rose from his chair. 'What are you doing, Abbie?'

'I've told Amos about his father, Edward. And I think he should see what Jim left for him and Seth and Sarah.'

Edward looked troubled. 'Are you sure this is right, Abbie?'

Abbie turned to him and sighed. 'He's eighteen, Edward. 'E should know. They should both know.'

She drew out a bag and another small package wrapped in cloth. Slowly she unrolled the cloth and handed the bag and package to Amos.

'The bag's for you and Seth and your mam,' said Abbie. 'And Jim said the other was for me.'

Amos set them on the table in the middle of the room. The bag was heavy and he looked inside it. Then he raised his eyes to Abbie's.

'It's money,' he said hoarsely. 'An' a lot of it, too.'

Abbie said nothing.

'Did 'e steal it?'

Abbie looked at the floor.

' 'E did, didn't 'e?'

'I . . . we can't be sure, Amos. But we think 'e did.'

Amos picked up one of the silver coins and turned it over in his hand. Then he let it drop back into the bag. Edward stood behind him, his arms folded. Amos could feel his disapproval, but he reached over and started undoing the package. Inside was a small gold snuffbox with a picture on the lid. He turned it over to look on the bottom. And, sure enough, there was another inscription. '*Presented to The Honourable Percy Fanshaw by his fellow officers.*' Percy Fanshaw! Lord Fanshaw's son.

Amos left the bag of money and the snuffbox lying on the table and then, without another word, he turned and walked out of the door.

Three months later

Edward was seldom angry, but he was this morning. He turned on Seth. 'Where's that brother of yours?' he demanded. 'He should 'ave bin 'ere an hour ago. I've got deliveries to make and there's that big order to finish.'

Seth twisted a piece of leather in his hands. ' 'E never

came home last night,' he said quietly. 'Mam's that worried about 'im.'

Edward looked up sharply. 'Do you know where he is, Seth?'

Seth shook his head.' 'E's bin acting strange for weeks. Restless, like. Honest, Uncle Edward, I dunno what's 'appened to him.'

For the rest of the day, there was so much work to be done that there was no time to wonder about Amos, but as Seth was helping to close the workshop, his uncle spoke again.

' 'Aven't you any idea where 'e is, Seth? 'E's your twin; 'e must've said sommat.'

Seth looked uncomfortable.' 'E's bin pretty quiet these past weeks; I've not got a lot from 'im; 'e just grunts when I speak to him – and 'e goes off on his own and doesn't tell us where.' He hesitated. ' 'E did once talk about getting a passage on one of them big sailing ships in the docks. But I thought it were just his talk. You know, Amos.'

Edward nodded grimly. 'And 'e said nothing else?'

Seth shook his head. 'No. I thought 'e'd stopped all that foolishness.'

Edward sighed. 'Go home now, boy, and look after your mam. I'll come round later to see her.'

Seth hurried away and Edward walked slowly back home. Abbie was already there. They looked at each other.

'There's bin nothing,' said Abbie. 'Not a word. Sarah's desperate.'

Edward nodded, then he sat down heavily. 'Abbie,' he said. 'Open the desk, will you.'

Abbie's eyes widened, but she said nothing. She found the key from the bunch at her waist and unlocked the bureau.

'You know what to look for,' said Edward.

She nodded.

She took out the heavy bag. But there was no sign of the package.

Edward heaved himself to his feet and came over. Abbie looked up at him and her eyes filled with tears.

'He's taken the snuffbox, Edward. And some of the money, too. How did he get to it? How did he unlock the desk?'

Edward shrugged. 'The key's not always at your waist, Abbie. You know that. So did Amos.' Edward put his hand into the bag of coins. 'He's taken what he thought was 'is share, I suppose.' Then he stopped and frowned, and then he opened the bag fully and looked inside. He drew out a piece of paper. 'It's a note,' he said quietly as he handed it to Abbie.

Abbie smoothed it out. 'It's for Seth,' she whispered.

'Read it out, Abbie.'

Abbie sniffed and cleared her throat. 'By the time you see this, I will be gone. I don't belong here any more. I've got a passage on a ship bound for Australia.

Don't think badly of me, Seth. I've only taken what is mine; the rest is for you and Mam. I'll send word when I get settled. Tell Mam I love her. Amos.'

Abbie broke down when she read the note and Edward put his arm round her to comfort her. But she didn't tell him what was really bothering her. Why had Amos taken the snuffbox? He knew that Jim had said it was for her. But, deep down, she wasn't so surprised. There had been a suspicion, long supressed; maybe Amos shared the suspicion. Maybe that's why he'd taken the snuffbox.

2

Donnelley's Creek, Victoria, Australia, 1864

Harriet Jones was twelve years old and she was not happy. She sat on the verandah of the hotel, in the rocker, and scowled as she pushed herself backwards and forwards. As she rocked, she stared out gloomily at the maze of forested ranges ahead.

What a harsh, grim place this was! Nothing but hostile bush, endless gum trees and rocky outctops and ravines. The settlement had been built here at Edwards Reef because gold had been discovered at nearby Donnelley's Creek two years ago. Her pa's hotel was here and so were all the other buildings that served Donnelley's, huddled together along the ridge.

Two years ago the new McEvoy track had been cut through from Gippsland. For some time, it had been known there was gold in these mountains and a few brave pioneers had spread stories about the place. But once the track was cut, packhorses and bullock teams could get through and people had rushed to Donnelley's

Creek from all corners of the world. The Irish, the English, the Chinese, the Germans. They came from everywhere; and they fought and they drank and they swore.

Harriet and her parents had come to Donnelley's early on. Her father and mother were hard-working folk. They'd been employed on a property near Melbourne when all the talk of gold began, and her father decided to take off and see if he could get a share of the wealth. He'd been canny – and he'd had some luck, too. As soon as gold was found, he'd staked his claim and had it properly registered back in the town of Sale, then he moved his family up here and they'd camped not far from where the hotel now stood. Most folk came here full of high hopes, then they spent back-breaking weeks and months panning and digging with precious little to show for it. And a lot of them took so long to register the claim they'd staked that others 'jumped' the claim and took it over.

Harriet and her family had seen the timber and bush cleared and a network of tracks cut to wherever gold had been discovered. Then great holes would be excavated and the creek beds disturbed as the diggers rushed to prospect for the precious gold they dreamt of day and night. Harriet had seen the first crushing machine brought in by bullock team from Port Albert and, along with all the other diggers, she and her family had watched anxiously the first trial crushings of the quartz.

Harriet remembered those first months, living in a canvas tenement, cooking on an open fire. She'd hated it, but her mother never complained. And she well remembered the day when her father had had his piece of luck . . .

He'd returned to the shack at midday, which was unusual. Her mother was giving Harriet her lessons – even in the harshest conditions, that was the rule. Every day, whatever else happened, Harriet did her reading and writing and sums. Her mother had stood up, alarmed.

'What's happened, Henry?'

Henry had reached out to his wife. 'Come here Molly,' he'd said softly, and for a few moments he had held her tight, smearing her clothes with mud. Then he'd grinned at them both, put his hand into the pocket of his breeches and held up a sizeable nugget of gold.

Harriet had let out a squeal of excitement and her hand had flown to her mouth. She well knew what this meant.

'Hush, girl,' said Henry quickly. 'Don't you tell a soul, d'you understand?'

'Where did you find it?' she asked.

'Just lying there, in a creek bed. After all the hacking and digging and crushing and panning. Can you believe it? It was there, twinkling back at me from under the water!'

'What will you do?' whispered Molly.

Henry kept his voice very low. 'I've thought it out, Molly. As luck would have it, no one was nearby when I found it, so no one knows but us. We must keep it that way.'

'You must get it somewhere safe,' said Molly. 'And get it valued.'

Henry nodded. 'This morning, I saw the rider coming up with the mail from Jordan. He'll stop here until tomorrow, then he'll ride back. I'll ride with him down to Jordan and get the nugget valued there.'

'What will we do with the money, Pa?' said Harriet.

Henry smiled at her. 'Let's just get the money in our hands, lass, before we do anything. And not a word to a living soul until we have.'

Molly and Harriet didn't need to be told again. They knew how rumours flew round the diggings. Men who boasted of a find were often set upon on their journey to sell their gold. Some were never seen again. It was best to keep as quiet as the grave.

'What will you tell folk? You'll have to have a reason for going all that way.'

Henry thought for a while. 'I'll say I've had word that my old mother's bin took bad.'

'Your mother died years ago!' said Molly.

'*We* know that, but no one else does.'

Molly had laughed. 'Now, give me that nugget, man, and I'll sew it into your other pair of breeches.

And you'd best get back to the diggings before you're missed!' . . .

All that had happened two years ago and, since then, Henry had used the gold money to build this hotel.

Harriet sniffed. Hotel! She'd been to Melbourne once and seen a real hotel. This was nothing more than a shack compared with the hotel in Melbourne. And as for the people that came here; they were the drunken loud-mouthed brawling diggers. They were dirty and quarrelsome and she kept out of their way as much as possible.

But sometimes there would by other visitors. Officials coming to look at the place to decide whether to set up a post office or the branch of a bank or a school. Her mother would cook for them and serve them such delicacies as wallaby, lyrebird and other native game.

Then there'd been the bad time, last year, when gold was discovered at Walhalla and the diggers had mostly left. The population at Edwards Reef dropped from one thousand to a few hundred. Most of the grog shanties closed down and Henry wondered whether he should give up, too. But he had hung on, and once the crushing machine arrived and the results of the trial crushings were good, the diggers had come back. Yet Henry knew it was a risky business. While the mountain still gave up its gold, while diggers flocked here, business was good – but it was anyone's guess how long it would last.

Harriet stood up and stretched. It was still early in the morning but already the harsh sun was beating down, striking through the gaps in the tall gums and picking up the dust motes floating in the air. A flock of brightly coloured rosellas flashed through the trees, breaking the silence of the bush, but Harriet hardly noticed them.

She *did* notice a man walking up from the canvas tenements towards the hotel. It was obvious that he was a digger, so she took no interest in him, though the diggers didn't usually come up to the hotel at this time of day. They set out early to work their claims, before the heat sapped their energy. Often they had a long way to walk through the hastily cut tracks, avoiding the thorns and prickles that snatched at them and keeping a lookout for the poisonous snakes which slithered across their path.

The man came nearer. He was dark and well-built but dirty, like all the diggers. She smoothed down her pinafore and waited for him to come up to her.

He stopped when he reached the verandah, but he didn't speak. He just looked Harriet up and down, unsmiling. Harriet felt uncomfortable.

'What do you want?' she asked, in her haughtiest voice.

The digger folded his arms. He didn't answer her question. Instead, he said, 'Who are you?'

Harriet was taken aback. 'I'm Harriet Jones,' she said frostily. 'My pa owns this hotel.'

The digger smiled then and Harriet was further unnerved.

'Does 'e now?' he said at last. 'Well, Harriet Jones,' he said, pronouncing the words very precisely, just as she had done, 'you tell your pa that I'd like to see 'im.'

Harriet folded her arms. 'What's your business?' she asked.

From inside the hotel, someone shouted Harriet's name. It was her mam, telling her to come and do her lessons.

Still the digger stood there.

'What's your business?' repeated Harriet. She was flustered now and blushing.

'I couldn't tell a chit of a girl like you my business, Harriet,' he said, continuing to smile.

To Harriet's relief, her mam came out on to the verandah then. 'Harriet, come along now,' she said, as she emerged from the cool darkness inside.

Harriet turned to her. 'Mam, this man wants to speak to Pa,' she said. 'And he won't say what he wants.'

Molly smiled. 'Perhaps he'll tell me,' she said gently. 'Now go on inside Harriet, and get your books out.'

With relief, and mustering what remained of her dignity, Harriet marched into the hotel, slamming the flimsy door behind her.

Molly turned to the digger, expectantly.

The man looked at her carefully. 'Are you Henry Jones' wife?' he asked.

Molly smiled. 'Indeed I am.'

A fleeting expression crossed the man's face, and if Molly hadn't been used to looking for signs of trouble, she would have missed it. It was an expression of pure hatred. She watched him carefully.

He had control of himself almost immediately. He coughed up some phlegm and spat it out on the ground, but Molly was not intimidated. She'd lived in this rough place for two years and she'd seen a lot.

'Tell your . . . husband,' said the digger, 'that I'd like to see him on urgent business.'

'Do you have a name?' persisted Molly.

The man looked up and met her eyes.

'My name,' he said loudly, 'is Amos Harris.'

Molly's expression didn't change, but Amos could see her hands clench at her sides. She knew who he was all right.

'Wait here, Mr Harris,' she said quietly. She walked slowly across the verandah and into the hotel, but as soon as she was inside she leant against the wall to steady herself. Then, taking a deep breath, she went to the back of the building where Henry was sitting at a table, counting up last night's takings. She stood behind him and put her hands on her shoulders.

'There's a young man outside you should see,' she said quietly.

Henry grunted. 'I'm busy,' he said.

'Henry, he says his name is Amos Harris.'

Bedford, present day, December

I haven't said anything to Mum, but I shall have to, soon. She knows something's bothering me. I expect she thinks I've had a row with Katie, or this bloke Tom who fancies me. I couldn't care less about Tom and I'd certainly never tell him anything about Matt, but I have told Katie what's happened and she's been really great.

Mum's going to find out soon though. Soon she'll try and get in touch with Matt. Things are going so well for Mum and I don't want to worry her. I want to find out where he is first and make sure he's okay.

I sent an email to the band's address yesterday, but there's been no reply. If only I could get rid of this feeling that something bad's happened. If only he'd just tell me where he is and what he's up to.

The next day

Well, Matt's been in touch! I was so relieved when I heard his voice. I blurted out all this stuff about thinking he'd gone missing again, and Mum, and why hadn't he told us he was moving, and was he coming home for Christmas etc etc. I banged on for so long that he had to cut me short. And when he spoke again, everything else that I was going to say just died on my lips.

'I'm in trouble, Becky,' he said.

I felt sick when he said, that. Matt never exaggerates. He's been in bad trouble before and if he says there's trouble, it's serious. I asked him what had happened, but he wouldn't give me a straight answer. He just told me he'd have to keep his head down for a while.

What does that mean, for God's sake?

Then he said something that completely threw me. 'Becky, it's to do with Keith.'

Keith! Mum's boyfriend who had caused Matt all that grief in the first place. What on earth could Keith have to do with anything? I thought he'd gone from our lives for ever.

Matt wouldn't say any more. Just said not to bother Mum and that he'd be in touch.

How can I keep it from Mum? She's bound to try and get hold of Matt soon. She'll want him here for Christmas.

And Keith! The thought of Keith coming back into our lives is just gross. Mum's moved on since then. She threw him out and I don't think she's ever regretted it. It was a bad time for all of us.

Donnelley's Creek, 1864

Henry stood up slowly and turned to face Molly. His face was deeply tanned but she could see how pale he had gone beneath the tan. He took her gently by the shoulders and looked straight into her eyes.

'It couldn't be him, could it?' he said, very quietly. ' 'Ere, in Donnelley's Creek. In this godforsaken backwoods place?'

Molly looked very frightened. 'I don't know. Mebbe it's just someone with the same name.'

' 'Ave you ever met another Amos in Victoria?'

Molly shook her head.

'If it is 'im,' said Henry slowly, 'then you know what he could do?'

Molly nodded. 'He could ruin us,' she whispered. 'All we've built up. Everything we've done together.'

Henry's eyes narrowed. 'He won't do that,' he said fiercely. 'Not while I have breath in my body he won't. He can't prove nothing; I'll not 'ave 'im come 'ere and interfere with my family.' He released Molly and shook his fist at the wall. 'I've dealt with plenty of rough diggers in my time. He'll be no different. I'll send 'im packing, Molly. I'll deny everything.'

Molly smiled at his defiance. 'That's the way, Henry. Now go and see 'im,' She hesitated. 'Mebbe 'e knows nothing anyway. Mebbe 'e's just looking for work in the hotel.'

Henry shrugged. 'Could be,' he said, but he didn't sound convinced. Then he frowned. 'If it *is* 'im,' he went on, 'then, in the name of all that's holy, how did he find us? That's what I can't understand.'

Molly put her hand up to Henry's cheek and stroked it. 'Nor me,' she said. 'You've been all over the state

33

and you've bin that careful; you've never let on to a living soul where you came from.'

'Aye,' said Henry, grimly. 'He'll 'ave 'ad a long search, that much is for sure.'

'Mam!'

It was Harriet, cross and querulous.

Molly went slowly to the door and called down the passage: 'I'm coming, dear.'

She looked back at Henry. 'Go on,' she said quietly. 'He's waiting out the front.'

Henry walked past her through the door, touching her hand briefly as he strode down the passage which led out to the verandah.

For a moment, Molly closed her eyes. 'Please God,' she prayed silently. 'Please God don't let him cause trouble for us.'

She heard Harriet slam a door and start walking down the passage. 'Mother!'

'I'm coming, dear. I'm coming now.'

Henry's heart was pounding in his chest as he went outside. Opening the door on to the verandah, he blinked in the bright sunlight and then shaded his eyes to look for the stranger. A stranger who could shatter all their dreams if he was so minded.

Amos was sitting in the rocker. He got up lazily as Henry emerged from the hotel and, for a few agonising seconds, the two men looked at each other. Henry found it hard to read the expression in the young man's eyes; but it was certainly hostile, no doubt of that.

And there was no doubt, either, who it was. It *was* him. Henry knew him instantly. He tried to betray nothing and his face was blank, but inside he seethed with a mass of conflicting emotions.

'Yes?' he said, shortly.

'Are you Henry Jones?' said Amos.

'Yes.'

Amos looked at him steadily. He'd planned this moment for two years but now it was here, he could say nothing. It *was* him all right. Even after all this time, he knew him. He'd never been more sure of anything.

Henry continued to stand there, outwardly calm, with his arms folded. 'What do you want?' he asked, and his voice was harsh.

Confronted at last by the man he'd been searching for, Amos dropped his gaze. He was suddenly unsure. Up till now, *finding* him was what mattered. So what *did* he want now that he was here, standing only a few feet away from him?

And then, something happened which surprised them both. Amos was suddenly hit by a wave of emotion and, to his horror, he started to weep. All his pent up fury dissolved and all the frustration of the last two years was expressed in his shuddering sobs. He couldn't stop himself, although he wiped at his eyes fiercely with the back of his hand. He mustn't break down, not now, of all times. He was a grown man, a tough man. How could he behave like a mewling infant!

But for Henry, to see this weeping young man in front of him was like a dagger to his heart. If challenged, he had been going to bluff it out, deny any connection with the man, refuse to acknowledge him. But, seeing him weeping there in front of him, all his resolutions were blown away and he went over to him instantly and put an arm round his shoulder.

He was near to tears himself as he touched Amos.

'You'd better come inside,' he said, gruffly.

The two of them, both with their dark good looks, walked into the hotel. Henry led the way down to the back room. Silently, he cleared his papers from the table and drew up another chair. 'Sit down lad,' he said.

Amos sat down opposite Henry. His hands were trembling so much that he put them on his knees and gripped hard to steady them. Now that he was here, now that he had found him, he didn't know what to say, where to begin.

Still Henry said nothing, so, hesitantly, Amos began. 'I've brought sommat to show you,' he said.

Henry watched as, with shaking hands, Amos dug deep in the pocket of his breeches and brought out a package, still wrapped in cloth. He put it on the table between them.

Very slowly, Henry reached out and unwound the

36

cloth. He knew what he would find but still he gasped as he looked at it again.

The snuffbox lay between them. Henry turned it over and silently read the inscription: '*Presented to the Honourable Percy Fanshaw by his fellow officers.*'

'I brought it with me,' said Amos, 'in case you didn't know me.'

Henry looked at the young man in front of him. His own flesh and blood. His son, whom he'd not seen since Amos was six years old. But the faces of those two boys had been imprinted on his conscience ever since.

'I'd know you anywhere, Amos,' he said quietly. Then he continued, with a trace of a smile, 'It's like seeing myself as a youngster. Except you're better looking and your teeth 'aven't half rotted away!'

Then Henry got up and walked over to a chest in the corner of the room. He knelt down and opened the lid and dug deep inside for a few moments before drawing out another package. He came back to Amos and handed it to him.

Amos looked up. 'Is this the watch?'

Henry nodded. 'Aye, the watch that caused all the trouble. The watch I served six years for stealing.'

Amos unwrapped the package and put the watch carefully down on the table between them, beside the snuffbox.

'It's a fine piece,' said Amos, at last.

'Aye, but not worth the price I paid for it – six years of hell, and more besides.'

Amos nodded slowly.

Henry picked up the watch and wrapped it up again.

'You can 'ave it when I'm gone, Amos.' He smiled. 'Mebbe you'll make yer fortune 'ere and 'ave fine clothes. Then you can wear it across your chest like a gentleman.'

Awkwardly at first, and then with less restraint, they began to talk. Amos told his father how he had traced him. How he'd been through all the records to find out which ship he could have taken when he left London and how there was no one on the crew list called Jim Harris.

'But I'd guessed you'd change your name right away,' he said.

'More than once,' said Henry. 'I went through a good lot of names before I settled on Henry Jones.'

Amos nodded. Not having a constant name to follow had been the hardest thing. Jim had been so many different people.

'And then I 'ad a bit of luck. I found someone who'd sailed with you. Someone who survived the wreck.'

'Who was that?'

'The ship's cook. 'E remembered a man who 'elped him that sounded like you. It were a slim chance, but I reckoned that was you all right.'

Henry nodded. 'E was good to me, the cook. Though it were tough, that passage. But better than being flung in prison again.' Then Henry shifted in his seat and frowned. 'But I was listed as drowned, son. Did no one ever tell you?'

Amos nodded. 'Mam and Aunt Abbie knew. Some sailor came to visit them and told them.'

At the mention of Sarah and Abbie, Henry went quiet and dropped his gaze. Amos looked at him carefully, then he continued.

'But sommat Aunt Abbie said always bothered me about the drowning,' he said. 'She told me how you could swim like a fish.'

Henry looked up and nodded. 'Aye,' he said. 'My pa taught me, when 'e was a Thames waterman. 'E said it was important to learn to swim if I was to follow in 'is trade. And I took to it. I've always liked the water.'

'Not many sailors could swim, could they?'

Henry shook his head. 'Hardly any. But it was that what saved me. Most of the crew were terrified of that wild sea off the Victoria coast. They would 'ave drowned right away. A few were lucky and caught onto pieces of driftwood and were flung on the beach. I found a spar and I swam towards a cove round the shore.'

'And what happened then?'

'I hid in a cave there, then at nightfall, I climbed up the cliff. I tell you, son, it were murder; steep and sharp and covered with thorny bush, but I wanted to live so bad that I hardly felt the cuts and bruises.' Henry cleared his throat. 'At the top I were half dead from hunger and being battered by the sea and climbing the cliff. So I rested up during the day, then I walked at night. I wanted to get as far as possible from the wreck.'

'How did you live? What did you eat?'

Henry shrugged. 'I don't like to think back on it; it was a horrible time. Sometimes I went days without food. I ate wild berries; I staked out any properties I came across. I stole food where I could.'

'And then?'

'I kept going inland, away from the sea. Away from anyone who might take me for a sailor. And I picked up casual work here and there where people didn't ask questions – on properties, working with stock. Enough to keep body and soul together.'

Amos nodded. 'I did the same,' he said. 'When I got off the boat in Melbourne me and some other fellas took casual work wherever we could.'

'When did you start looking for me?'

'Right away,' said Amos. 'I never believed you'd drowned. Wherever I went, I asked if they'd seen you or heard of you, but it was 'ard with all the times you changed your name. I'd describe you as best I could and most folk 'adn't heard of you, but then, every now and again I'd be working on a property where someone remembered someone who sounded like

40

you. Someone you'd spoken to about your pa being a Thames waterman. Little things like that.'

'It would have bin a long trail,' muttered Henry.

Amos nodded. 'Two years,' he said flatly. 'For two years, I've followed up any casual sighting, a chance remark. And mostly they led to nothing.'

'But you never gave up.'

Amos shook his head and, for a long moment, father and son stared at each other. Amos saw a once-handsome man, with a lean, wiry body, a lined and weatherbeaten face and not many teeth in his head. The expression was wary but there was no anger there now. But his life had hardened him. He was a tough fellow, that much was certain.

And, in Amos, Henry simply saw himself as a young man, angry and full of resentment. But why, he wondered, *why* should Amos be angry and bitter? He'd not been imprisoned for a crime he didn't commit. He'd probably had it easy, with Abbie and her dull Edward to look out for him. What had driven him to come to Australia? Was it *just* his conviction that his father was still alive?

Henry cleared his throat. 'Do they know where you are? Does your mam know where you are?'

Suddenly Amos's eyes flashed with anger as he thought of Sarah. 'Of course they do. And how dare you speak of Mam!' he shouted. 'You abandoned 'er and left 'er to grovel in the streets for food and forced 'er to come on 'er knees to beg Aunt Abbie to care for us.'

Henry looked at the floor. 'I'm not proud of what I did, son,' he said quietly. 'But it was better that way.'

'Better!'

Henry nodded. 'Better for your mam to think I was dead,' he said. 'We were no good for each other. She maddened me and I maddened 'er.'

Amos scraped his chair back and stood leaning over his father. 'You were 'er husband!' he shouted.

Henry flinched, then raised his eyes slowly and looked his son full in the face.

'No, Amos. We were never wed. We were never man and wife.'

For a moment, Amos stood stock still, staring at his father.

'Then I'm nothing to you!' he said quietly. 'I'm just your bastard – and that whey-faced prissy little Miss outside is your legal spawn?'

Henry's chin jerked back as if he'd been physically hit. He clenched his fists, but he didn't raise his voice when he replied.

'Yes. Molly and I are wed,' he said quietly, 'and Harriet is our daughter.'

For answer, Amos turned his face away and spat contemptuously on the floor.

Henry looked at his son and felt torn apart. His new family was that precious to him, he'd do anything to protect them. But he understood Amos, too. He well understood his fury and hatred, and he would have to tread very very carefully with him. If he had a mind to, Amos could ruin everything, even now, after all these years.

The law had a long memory.

Henry stood up and went across to Amos. He put out a hand to touch his shoulder, but Amos shrugged it away.

'Don't touch me, damn you!'

There was a tense silence just filled with the breathing of the two men, then Henry spoke.

'Amos, you are my son. You've always bin my son and there's not a day gone by when I've not thought about you and Seth.'

'Don't try and soften me with your lies,' hissed Amos, turning back towards his father.

'I swear it's true,' said Henry, quietly.

'And Mam?' said Amos, his eyes narrowing. 'You've thought of her every day too, I suppose? That's why you upped and married someone else!'

Henry dropped his gaze. 'I told you, son. Sarah and I were never right for each other. I could never 'ave made 'er 'appy.'

'And this *wife* of yours. This woman who's taken Mam's rightful place. You can make 'er 'appy I suppose?'

'Yes,' said Henry simply.

For a moment, Amos was thrown by the certainty in Henry's voice. Then he cleared his throat.

'And now, I've turned up like a bad penny to upset your cosy home,' he said bitterly, meeting his father's eyes. 'I wonder what Miss prissy Harriet would say if she knew she had a bastard half-brother?'

There was a long silence, then Henry said, as evenly as he could manage, 'I can't stop you telling 'er, Amos, and to be honest, out here in the bush no one would care. It's day-to-day survival that counts 'ere, not whether you're wed or not. But I would ask you not to tell Harriet. Not yet, at least. It would be cruel, you must see that.'

When Amos didn't answer, Henry went on. 'She's a dreamer, Amos. She wants to be a grand lady and get away from this rough life. But she's only young. Life'll be real for her soon enough.'

Still Amos didn't answer. Henry sighed.

'Stay here awhile, Amos, please. Now you've found me. Give us all a chance to get to know each other.'

Amos suddenly gripped the back of the chair and lifted it off the ground as if to attack Henry, but Henry stood his ground.

'Aren't you scared of me?' whispered Amos. 'I could ruin you.'

'No son, I'm not scared of you,' said Henry. 'I'm sorry for you. And I'm sorry what I did to you and Seth and your mam. I know you could ruin me, ruin what I've worked for and built up here, but my whole life's been a gamble, Amos. I'm used to running and, if necessary, I'd run again.'

Amos didn't answer. He let the chair drop and then he turned and walked outside. He looked around him at the wild country, ripe for taming, then he sat down on the edge of the verandah and buried his head in his arms.

This time he didn't want anyone to see him cry.

For the first few weeks that Amos lived at Edwards Reef, the tension was almost unendurable. Henry and Molly welcomed him to the hotel whenever he chose to come, but Harriet couldn't understand why this rough man was given free meals and drink. She had hated him on sight and she hated him more and more as he taunted her without mercy, making her redden furiously and squirm with embarrassment.

But Henry had sensed a curiosity in Amos about the hotel and gradually, he started talking to Amos about it, telling him a little of how it was run, the problems with supplies, how it all depended on whether the gold was still being found and if it wasn't, how the miners would leave Edwards Reef and go elsewhere.

And, despite himself, Amos found himself drawn into the day-to-day ebb and flow of the business.

As for Molly, she tried her best to keep the peace between Harriet and Amos, but it wasn't easy. She understood Harriet's jealousy and confusion at her father's sudden interest in this roughly spoken stranger, but she was desperate to make Amos welcome, for his father's sake – for all their sakes.

To begin with, Amos simply ignored Molly, or only

answered her gruffly and rudely. But then, when Molly never responded angrily, he softened to her just a bit, though he could never forget that she had taken his mam's place.

And, despite himself, he had to admire the way in which she took her share of running the hotel, the way she organised the food, kept the place clean, dealt with difficult customers.

It was a couple of months after his arrival, when Henry and Amos had been working all day unloading supplies and checking them, that they sat down together for a drink as the sun set behind the trees.

'Amos,' said Henry suddenly, 'I'd like to tell you about Molly.'

Instantly, Amos was on his guard. 'Why?'

'Because I want you to understand,' said Henry.

And, although at first Amos turned his head away, feeling guilt and disloyalty to his mam, slowly he started listening. Listening to a compelling and unlikely love story. He heard how Molly and his father had met while they were both working on a big property in Victoria. How she had changed his life, calmed him, soothed all the hate and resentment. In short, she had turned his life around.

'Her folk didn't want us to wed,' said Henry, smiling. 'And who could blame them? I was feckless and unreliable, I'd been in prison, I'd wandered from job to job. I had no legal papers.'

'Did they know who you were? Your real name?'

Henry shook his head. 'Her folk don't know. But I have no secrets from Molly.'

Amos dropped his gaze. 'I need to write home,' he announced suddenly.

Henry's head jerked up. 'Will you say owt to Abbie and your mam when you write?' he said anxiously. 'About finding me and that?'

'I dunno,' said Amos. 'I need to think.'

'It won't solve aught,' said Henry, quietly. 'It would just stir things up.' Then he went on, choosing his words carefully, 'Amos, if you've a mind to, you could help me here. Help me properly, I mean, and have a stake in the business. Things are going well but we need to think ahead; we should build another hotel.'

Amos looked up. 'Are you asking me to help you just to keep an eye on me, to keep me quiet, stop me from telling your secrets?' he said harshly.

Henry looked back at him steadily. 'No, Amos, I'm asking you to help me because you're my son and because I think you 'ave a feel for the business.'

Then, when Amos didn't reply, he added quietly. 'And I trust you.'

3

Donnelley's Creek, December 1865

Henry and Amos were hunched over a pile of papers in the back room of the hotel, trying to make sense of columns of figures. Amos was good at arithmetic, but Henry had only been taught the rudiments and he was slower to grasp what figures meant.

The last year had been filled with activity at Edwards Reef. A great number of buildings had gone up, including a post office, police quarters, stables and a lock-up. A Justice of the Peace had been appointed to preside over minor court cases, the Bank of Victoria had opened an agency and there was now a private school to serve the children of better-off miners and storekeepers living on the reef.

And Henry had built a second hotel. It had only been opened a couple of months and already he was regretting his rashness.

'I should've known, son. One minute you're riding on

the hog's back and then the next, the gold is gone and the miners are up and off to the next place.'

It was true. The old hotel had been full to bursting every night, but, now, because of lack of water, the creek gold was getting harder to find. Just as the new hotel had opened, there'd been rumours of a big find at Stringers Creek and the mining population took off, dwindling overnight from over one thousand to a couple of hundred.

'It's the drought,' said Henry gloomily. 'If the drought would only break then the creeks would fill again and they'd find the alluvial gold.'

'Will they come back once the drought breaks?' asked Amos.

Henry shrugged. 'Who knows? Depends how good it is at Stringers.'

Amos scraped back his chair and locked his hands behind his head.

'You should sell up and buy sommat where the population is steady. In some town that doesn't rely on gold. It's too fickle.'

Henry nodded. 'Easier said than done, Amos. We'll have to hang on here now. No one's going to buy the property if it's not a going concern.'

'I know. I realise that. But, if the miners come back. If things start going well. Then's the time to sell up.'

Henry rubbed his chin. 'Mebbe,' he said uncertainly.

'It's the only way to make money,' said Amos eagerly.

'Doing business out here in the bush is all ups and downs. We should think big. Go somewhere where's there's always lots going on.'

Henry smiled. 'You do me good, Amos. You've got vision, son.'

Amos leaned forward. 'Will you promise me to sell, once the hotels are going well again?'

'I can't promise you anything, Amos,' said Henry firmly, showing the tough side which Amos had come to respect over the past year.

'At least think about it?'

Henry nodded. 'If things get better, then I promise I'll think about it,' he said. 'Molly could do with an easier life,' he said quietly. Then he grinned. 'And young Harriet would like living in a town,' he said.

Amos snorted. 'Young Harriet's too big for those fancy boots of hers,' he said. 'Sneering at the rest of us, putting on airs and graces. She could do with a good slap.'

'Don't be so hard on her, Amos,' retorted Henry angrily. 'She's had a lot to put up with.'

'You mean me?'

Henry looked awkward. 'You know she finds it hard to understand why I've taken you on,' he said. 'Why I rely on you and trust you and give you responsibility.'

'Then mebbe it's time you told her who I was?'

'No. Not yet a while.'

* * *

But it was getting harder. Harriet was fiercely jealous of Amos.

'Why is Pa always with him?' she asked her mother. 'That Amos is going to take over the business, I can see it coming. He'll cheat us all!'

'Hush, Harriet,' said Molly wearily. 'Amos has been a great help to your pa. Surely you can see that?'

'Huh! Great help indeed. Getting him to build another hotel which is standing empty.'

Molly frowned. 'No one could know about the drought, dear, nor about the find at Stringers Creek.'

Harriet narrowed her eyes. 'He's rude and rough and I don't like him.'

Molly sighed. 'Harriet,' she said. 'Your pa and I love you. You know that. Pa wouldn't do aught to harm you or take anything away from you.'

Harriet shrugged and looked uncomfortable.

Molly went on. 'I'll have a word with Amos.'

'*No*, Mam! I don't want him to think he riles me.'

'Well, dear,' said Molly gently, 'You two are just going to have to learn to get along. I'm afraid Amos is here to stay.'

Harriet stared at her mother. Having it said out loud really shocked her. So he was going to stay. He was going to be a part of her life. She'd never be free from his teasing and sarcastic jibes.

It was horrible! She couldn't bear it!

Harriet burst into tears and stormed out of the room.

Molly bit her lip and frowned. Poor Harriet. It was so hard on the child. Perhaps she should be told who Amos was? But then, Henry would have to explain everything to her. How he'd been transported from London for theft, imprisoned at Point Puer, made his way as a thief back in London, changed his name and returned to Australia.

No, the child couldn't be told yet. Let her dream her dreams. Why should they shatter them for her?

Molly went after her and found her slumped at the foot of a tall gum tree at the back of the hotel. She crouched down beside her and stroked her hair.

'Don't take on so, love. Please don't take on so.'

Bedford, present day, January

It was a miserable Christmas. Matt rang Mum to say he couldn't come home. He made up some story about going to friends. It isn't that. Of course it isn't. He doesn't want to come home because Keith might find him here. Even though we've moved house, we're in the phone book. It wouldn't take long to track us down. Matt doesn't want Keith causing trouble here; and he doesn't want Mum to know anything about him being in trouble.

Mum was cool about it — on the outside, anyway. She said that at least he'd let us know about Christmas. But she was so disappointed. She tried to hide it, but I could tell. And she's confused, too. She's tried to phone his flat a few times; I've told her he's moved and the new flat hasn't got a phone yet, but she's started to guess that things aren't right.

Gran and Grandad came on Christmas Day and I tried to make it good for Mum. She put on a brave face but it wasn't special, somehow. It would have been really special if Matt had been there.

Bloody Keith! Why is Matt so scared of him?

Well, tomorrow I hope I'll find out. I've told Mum that Katie and me are going to the January sales in London. We will, too, but I've arranged to meet up with Matt later.

It's horrible, lying to Mum like this. I wish I could tell her. Maybe after tomorrow I'll be able to.

The next day

It's worse than I thought. I'm really scared for Matt now.

We met in this little café behind Oxford Street. It would have been fun if I hadn't been so worried. Matt was late, but that's nothing new. Eventually he came shambling in.

He looked terrible. Pale and gaunt and furtive somehow.

I'd chosen a table by the window, but as soon as he sat down, he said he wanted to move to the back. I suppose he was scared of being seen. It was really spooky.

He seemed anxious about Mum and he kept asking about her – about her job, whether she'd got another bloke, that sort of *stuff. I told him she was doing great. That she had a lot of new friends, that she was really enjoying her job and that no, there wasn't any special bloke in her life.*

He seemed relieved then.

At last, I couldn't stand it any longer. 'What is it, Matt?' I blurted out. 'What's happened?'

So he told me. Slowly at first, talking very quietly so I could hardly hear him.

It seems that Keith works for some loan shark outfit; a company that lends money to very poor people, people who've got into debt and have nowhere to turn. The company offers to lend them money, but then demands huge repayments. And if the people don't pay, they send round the heavy mob to scare them or to take away their furniture and their tellys and videos. They strip their houses while the wretched people stand and watch, not able to do a thing.

Well, somehow Keith had heard about Matt's band, so he got in touch via their website and offered to finance them so they could buy some special equipment and make more CDs and stuff.

'It sounded good, Becky,' said Matt.

'But KEITH!'

'Oh, give me a break, Becky. If I'd known Keith was involved, I wouldn't have touched it. He didn't do it himself; he got another bloke to do it. Keith's name was never mentioned . . . until we'd signed the deal.'

'We were stupid, Becky. We thought we'd soon get the money back and be able to repay the loan. We didn't read

the small print. And I was the one that signed all the papers.'

'Why did they approach you in the first place?' I asked.

He shrugged. 'Don't suppose they would have if it hadn't been for Keith, the devious bastard. He's found a way to mess things up for me. He hates me, Becky, you know that. He always blamed me for setting Mum against him. Well, he's found a way to get back at me and this is how. While I was still at the flat, he phoned all the time, telling me to get the money or else. He's loving it, Becky. He's loving making me squirm. He's a psycho, Becky. He's twisted.'

I was really shocked at this. I'd never liked Keith. He'd almost split the family apart, but this was different. This was planned and sadistic. The man was unbalanced.

'How did he find out about the band?' I asked.

Matt shrugged. 'I suppose someone must've told him. I expect he still has a few contacts in Bedford. Someone must've said I'd come good. Matt laughed harshly. 'That wouldn't have pleased him much. I expect he'd hoped I'd be dead or a hopeless crackhead sleeping rough under a bridge.'

'So you really think he's gone to all this trouble to try and crush you?'

Matt nodded. 'He's a vicious bastard. He's determined to get back at me. I've had to drop out of college, Becky. Leave the flat. And we can't do any gigs because Keith's heavies would be there to seize the equipment.'

'So you can't repay the money.'

Matt shook his head. 'If the repayments were a sensible amount and we had the time, we'd probably be okay. But as it is, we're stuffed, Becky. We need five grand and every day we don't repay, the debt goes up.'

My mouth dropped open then. Five thousand pounds!

He just sat staring at me, slumped in his seat at the table in the café.

Then he'd made me promise not to tell Mum. He's scared that any mention of Keith will upset her too much.

I wish I hadn't made that promise. I can talk to Katie about it, but I really need to talk to someone older. Someone who could tell me what to do. Who to go and see.

Matt needs help. And he needs it fast.

And then, when I was thinking about it at home, I started wondering about why Keith had done this. Does he just want to hurt Matt or does he want to get at me and Mum, too?

Is he screwed up enough to think like that?

What if he sends his heavies round here to scare me and Mum?

4

Donnelley's Creek, April 1866

Henry stood on the verandah of the new hotel and breathed in deeply. In March, the long drought had broken at last and the hard earth had softened. The creeks were running with water again and the diggers were returning. Mining and crushing operations were getting back to full strength and both hotels were full of customers.

It was early morning and Henry looked out over the bush; there was an acrid smell of smoke which rose from the fires around the diggers' camp and, now that the dusty heat of summer was gone, this came through more strongly even than the all-pervading smell of eucalypt from the gum trees.

It was a tough landscape, out here. Tough and wild and hostile. If Edwards Reef was finally deserted by the fickle mining population, the bush would soon reclaim it and there'd be nothing to show for the seething mass which was here now, digging and panning, living and hoping, swearing and quarreling. Nothing but headstones in the graveyard outside the settlement. But even they would be swallowed up in a year or so. Nature would have the last say.

But for now, Henry was almost content. They were making money again – for the moment. Though, the more he thought about it, the more Henry was convinced that Amos was right. Give it a bit longer; let folk forget the bad times – and then sell up.

He stretched his arms above his head and yawned loudly, thinking to the future. With Amos to help him, he felt more confident. They were very alike, father and son; they both wanted to better themselves, to move on, to grab opportunities when they arose. They had their differences and, at first, Amos often flared with anger when he thought back to what Henry had done to his mam, but gradually, as he got to hear more, during their late-night talks, he had come to understand what had happened in the past, though he could never forget the hurt it had caused. Henry was grateful to Amos, too. Grateful that he'd not told Abbie and Sarah his story. Amos wrote home describing everything and saying how he was working for a man called Henry Jones, so he was telling them no lies. But he never told them that Henry Jones was Jim Harris, the father, brother and husband they all thought was dead.

As Henry surveyed the scene before him, he saw the rider with the mailbag urging his horse up the track towards the settlement. At first light, he would have set out from Jordan, one of the staging posts on the route of the Victorian Express. Idly, Henry watched as the man dismounted at the post office, tethered his horse outside, heaved the mailbag off the horse and walked inside the building. Later, a whistle would be blown to alert the miners that the mail was ready for collection.

It was a marvel, thought Henry, what services there were out here, deep in the bush. 1866 was proving a good year; everything was expanding and things were going very well.

But for how long?

Harriet came out onto the verandah, dressed ready to go to school. Henry looked at her. She was fourteen and growing up fast. She was quite the young lady now, and he often wondered what the future held for her. His heart went out to her. He loved her deeply, but her airs and graces irritated folk. It seemed she was never satisfied. He sighed. Maybe one day she'd marry some city fellow; maybe that would make her happy. He smiled at her and, briefly, she smiled back, a genuinely warm smile. But then Amos appeared and the smile vanished.

'Off to yer fancy school then, Harriet?' Amos said.

She didn't reply. The school was certainly not fancy, and Amos knew that very well. Lessons were taught by a schoolmarm in her house, which was not much more than a shack and was cramped and smelly. Harriet longed to go to an elegant school in a big town. Not that she'd ever seen such a school, but she could dream. She was sick of rubbing shoulders with the loutish girls who were daughters of storekeepers or of miners who had struck lucky.

But at least she was learning about things that were important to her – things like manners and etiquette. Things other folk round here knew nothing of. There were no social graces out here in the bush.

She walked off down the track, looking straight ahead, ignoring Amos, who stood, with his arms folded, looking after her and grinning.

It was getting worse, this bad feeling between Harriet and Amos, and it saddened Henry.

'Don't rile her so, Amos,' he said, mildly.

Amos spat on the ground. 'Huh! 'She makes me wild, the little madam. One day, I swear I'll put her over my knee and wallop her good and proper.'

Henry rounded on him. 'You're a lot older than her,' he said angrily. 'Give the lass a chance, will you?'

Harriet's behaviour was something they couldn't discuss rationally. Their opinions on young Harriet were poles apart.

Amos had the good sense to change the subject. 'There's a big delivery coming up the track today. Do you want me to deal with it?'

Henry shook his head. 'I'll see to it, son. You take a break for a while.'

Amos didn't need telling twice. Life in the bush wasn't sophisticated, but it did have its pleasures. There were plenty of lusty women on the settlement and Amos was a good-looking young man. While the men were at the diggings, there was sport to be had!

Henry knew this only too well and it put him in mind of his own careless ways back in London. But one day, he thought, if Amos wasn't very careful, he'd find himself in serious trouble. One day, he'd get his comeuppance for all this wenching.

All the more reason for moving on, going to a big town before Amos was set upon by the angry father or brother of some lass he'd had his way with, before there was a bastard baby on the way.

Amos ran his hand through his hair and tucked his shirt into his breeches. 'I'll be off, then,' he said.

Henry nodded. 'Call in at the post office later, Amos. The rider's just come. See if there's any mail for us.'

Amos raised his arm in reply and ran off down the track.

Henry went inside. He walked into the kitchen, where Molly was preparing some poultry for dinner.

'Amos riles Harriet all the time,' he said to Molly. 'He won't leave 'er alone. Whenever he sees her, he teases her and she can't abide it.'

Molly nodded. 'I know, and my heart bleeds for 'er. She's not bin used to teasing and she can't 'andle it. But there's nowt we can do about it, Henry, except try and get Amos to stop, but 'e says its doing 'er no 'arm and she's bin spoilt.' Molly dried her hands on a clout, thoughtfully and then she picked up another bird to pluck. 'And 'e may 'ave a point, I suppose. Being the only one, mebbe we *'ave* spoilt Harriet.' She held the dead bird away from her and began to pull skilfully at its feathers. 'But they're never going to get on, those two. They're like chalk and cheese.'

There was an easy silence between them for a few moments, then Henry stroked his chin. 'I've bin thinking, Molly. We need to move on soon. Things are really good now and we should sell up before the next slump and set up somewhere else.'

Molly looked at him and sighed, thinking of the upheaval. Then she smiled. 'It's good to 'ear you talk like that, Henry, after the bad times we've 'ad, the drought and all. But where would we go?'

'To Melbourne.'

Molly's nimble fingers froze in the act of plucking the bird.

'Melbourne! You mean start up a hotel there?'

Henry nodded.

'That'd cost a fair bit. We'd 'ave to borrow.'

'I know, Molly. I know. But it's the way forward – and I've got Amos to help me now. He's hungry for work, he's ambitious and he's full of good sense, despite his rough ways.'

'Yes,' she said slowly.' I know he is. I can see that. And, perhaps if he had more to think about, he'd stop pestering Harriet.'

'And all the other women on the settlement, too!' muttered Henry.

Molly smiled. 'He's a good looker, I'll give him that. Just like his dad!'

Henry took Molly's hand. 'Well, I only 'ope for his sake that he finds a wife like you one day.'

'Get along with you, Henry Jones!' Then, frowning, she said. 'If you're to rely on Amos so much in future, mebbe we should get the doctor to take a look at him, make sure he's in good health before you go giving him all this work to do. Remember that bad turn he had a couple of months back?'

'I'll never forget it,' said Henry. 'On the morning of Harriet's fourteenth birthday.'

'Aye, the twentieth of March . . .'

That morning, Amos had woken suddenly, very early, choking and gasping for breath. He'd staggered to Henry for help, shouting out that he was dying, and Henry and Molly had looked on helplessly as his lips had turned blue and he'd gulped for air and thrashed about on the floor at their feet. Then, as suddenly as it had started, the seizure had stopped. Amos had taken some deep, shuddering breaths and got shakily to his feet. But the incident had frightened him; and it had frightened Henry and Molly.

Harriet had been frightened, too. But for a different reason. Woken by all the noise, she'd got out of bed and pattered down the passage. She'd heard Amos yell out that he couldn't breathe, that he was dying.

And she was pleased.

For a few moments, she thought he would go from their life for ever; and she felt a surge of pure joy go through her.

And then she felt guilty – and frightened, too, at the strength of her emotion. There was no doubt that she had wanted him dead . . .

Henry let go of Molly's hand. 'But it were just the once,' he said. 'There's bin nothing since then. He seems as strong as an ox.'

'He does that,' said Molly. 'But anyways, 'e's twenty-four now. It's time he stopped all this womanising and found a wife.'

'I'll send him to Melbourne, Molly. That'll keep him occupied. He can see if he can find a buyer for the properties up here.'

'And find a wife?' smiled Molly.

'Aye. And mebbe find a wife, too!'

Henry walked towards the door. 'That delivery should be coming up the track some time this morning. Keep your eyes open for it and tell me when it's in sight.'

It arrived mid morning and for the next couple of hours, Henry and his helpers were busy unpacking foodstuffs, tools, materials and all sorts of other supplies and checking them against their lists. It was dinner time before they had finished.

At dinner time, Harriet headed back to the hotel for her meal. She put her books tidily into her bag, smoothed down her pinafore and patted her hair, then she left the school house and walked towards the hotel. Earlier, when she'd peered out of the window during a lesson, she had glimpsed Amos kissing a girl behind one of the big gum trees just beside the school house. Harriet had sniffed in disapproval, blushed deeply and turned back to her books. The incident had unsettled her; Amos was a disgrace and she was ashamed to have anything to do with him. She still felt angry and upset when she set off for home.

But what happened next drove all other thoughts from her head.

There was a sudden loud cry. It came from outside the hotel; it was a man's voice and it was a shout of raw anguish.

Harriet quickened her pace, her heart thudding. But when she came in sight of the hotel, she stopped, suddenly unsure.

Standing on the verandah, her father and Amos were locked in an embrace and they were both weeping. Amos had a letter clutched in his hand.

Harriet approached slowly and stood below the verandah, looking up. Neither man noticed her.

'Whatever's the matter?' she asked shrilly.

The moment the words left her lips, she knew she had said the wrong thing. Even *she* could hear the querulous tone, the disapproval. She hadn't meant it to sound like that, but she was scared. She'd never seen a man cry before.

But it was too late. The damage had been done.

Wrenching himself away from his father, Amos rounded on Harriet.

'I'll tell you what's the matter, you stupid stuck up little bint!' he yelled at her.

'Amos!' shouted Henry. 'That's enough. Stop it, at once!'

But Amos was blinded by grief and fury.

'I'll tell you what's the matter,' he shouted. 'My twin has drowned! My lovely brother, Seth, who never harmed a fly in his entire life. He's drowned in the River Thames and he's left behind a young wife and a baby boy.'

Harriet hung her head. She knew nothing of Amos's family.

Henry grabbed Amos's arm, but Amos shook it off.

'And do you want to know why your father is so upset? Well, I'll tell you, Harriet. He's so upset because Seth was his son.'

'Oh God, Amos, why . . .' began Henry. Then he stopped and, for a moment, there was complete silence between them all. The only noise came from the distant thump of the crushing machine and the squawks of the rosellas in the trees.

Harriet couldn't take it in. She looked to her father to deny it, but his head was bent..

'What do you mean?' she said.

'I mean,' said Amos, quieter now, but his voice still full of venom, 'that Seth was your half-brother.'

'I don't understand,' she stammered.

'It's not difficult,' said Amos, his voice heavy with sacasm. 'Especially for a young girl of learning like you.'

'Please, Amos, *don't*,' said Henry.

'What's he mean, Father?' repeated Harriet.

'It's simple, Harriet,' said Amos. 'Your father had another life before he came to Australia; and another family. Seth was his son.'

'And Seth was your twin?' whispered Harriet.

'Seth was my twin, so I'm your half brother, God help me.'

Harriet took a moment to absorb this shattering fact.

'What happened to your mother, then?' she said at last, but still with that peevish tone that Amos so loathed.

'My mother, Sarah, is alive and well, Harriet.'

Harriet's eyes widened.

Amos shot a quick glance at Henry. 'But your father never wed her, so I'm a bastard. Your bastard half-brother.'

Harriet flinched at the word bastard and Henry put his head in his hands and groaned.

Molly had come through from the back of the hotel and had been listening in horror. She went first to Henry and held him close. Then she walked over to Harriet, put an arm around her and led her away inside.

Henry wiped his eyes and straightened his shoulders. Amos looked at him and suddenly the anger left him. 'I'm sorry,' he muttered.

Henry turned on him, furiously. 'How *dare* you speak to her like that!' he hissed. 'It was cruel and unnecessary!' He ran his shaking hands through his hair. '*I* could have told her in my own way, but not like *that*. It was *vicious*, Amos. *Vicious*. I'm ashamed of you!'

And this time, it was Amos who hung his head. There was a long and heavy silence between them. At last Amos held the letter out to Henry. 'Do you want to read it?' he said hoarsely.

Henry shook his head. 'No. You read it out to me.'

So Amos read the letter from Sarah. His heart turned over as he saw again the ill-formed script. His mother had never had much schooling and Abbie would have helped her as she painstakingly scratched away to give him the dreadful news. All his letters from Sarah had been written with Abbie's help; Amos knew that.

The letter was short and factual. It recounted how Seth had been driving the horse and cart beside the river, coming back from delivering an order, when a bolting horse had crashed into him. His own horse had lost its footing and it and the cart had landed in the water. Seth had been trapped in the water, under the cart.

But it was the last line that tugged at Amos's heartstrings: *'So now I have lost both my sons.'*

Amos finished reading and looked at Henry. 'I must go to her,' he said quietly.

Henry nodded. 'Yes, you must.' He sighed. 'I'll pay for your passage, son,' he added quietly.

Amos swallowed. 'But I'll be back, Father.'

It was the first time he had called him father.

Henry looked up sharply and Amos nodded in confirmation. 'No more pretending.'

'No. I suppose there's no need now. At least not between ourselves.'

Then, standing there, on the verandah, in the noonday sun, Henry told Amos of his plans to sell up at Edwards Reef and buy a hotel in Melbourne and how he needed Amos to help him.

'I'll go to Melbourne right away,' said Amos. 'It'll take a while to get a passage back to London, so I'll use the time to look for a buyer for the hotels.'

'And you promise you'll come back?'

'My future's here with you,' said Amos. 'I swear I'll come back.'

Henry met his son's eyes. 'I believe you, son.'

For a while, neither spoke, both too full of thoughts and emotion. Then Henry turned to go inside to join

Molly and Harriet. At the door, he stopped. 'What day did you say Seth died?'

Amos took a deep breath, then he said slowly, 'He died on the evening of the nineteenth of March.'

Henry started. 'The evening before Harriet's birthday! And you had that turn the next morning, when it would have been evening back in London.'

'Yes. The time I thought I was choking to death. The time when I couldn't breathe.'

'They say one twin always knows when sommat's amiss with the other one.'

'Aye,' said Amos, hoarsely. 'That's what they say.'

Bedford, present day, January.

I saw Keith today! I couldn't believe it. There he was, large as life and twice as horrible, leaning against a wall, talking into his mobile.

It was in the town centre, and just for a moment, I froze. Then I darted into a shop to hide. I didn't get to see him for long, but I know it was him. I'd recognise him anywhere. He looked terrible – madder than ever. Wild, with bulgy eyes.

What's he doing here? Has he come to spy on us? Is he trying to find Matt?

I'm going to have to tell Mum now. She'll be scared out of her wits, but it's better she's warned. What'll happen if she bumps into him in town?

Two days later

I've finally plucked up the courage to tell her and now I wish I'd done it earlier, although Matt'll be furious with me. I thought she'd be really scared, but she was more angry than anything else.

She's changed, has Mum. When Keith first met her, just after Dad died, she was timid and unsure. I suppose she thought she needed Keith to look after her.

Well, she's not like that any more, that's for sure! She's doing fine on her own and she's a lot stronger.

When I told her what Keith was doing to Matt, she went ballistic!

'How dare he!' she said. Then she said a lot more and went on saying it for a very long time.

When she'd calmed down, she got on the phone to a lawyer friend of hers and explained what had happened. But when she got off the phone, she was very upset. Still angry, but really down.

'The bastard!' she said. 'I can't believe what he's doing is legal.'

'Is it?' I'd asked.

She'd nodded. 'Apparently, just as long as the paperwork's been signed and there's no evidence of physical violence, there's nothing the law can do to stop it because Matt's eighteen now.'

Then she went on, chatting to me like I was her friend. It was strange; it was the first time I felt we were talking as adult to adult.

'He's ill, Becky. Keith's mentally ill. I only realised after I'd been with him some time, because it's borderline, but it's obviously got worse. He's jealous and obsessive and if someone turns against him or defies him, he's like a mad bull.'

I nodded, remembering the shouting matches between him and Matt, before Matt left home, and then my glimpse of him looking wild in the town centre.

'I've been dreading something like this,' Mum went on. 'He'll have been brooding all this time, thinking of ways to get back at us. Biding his time. If only he'd got professional help. I tried to get him to see a doctor when he was living with us, but he refused to admit that anything was wrong with him.'

'Can't we do something to stop him doing this to Matt?'

Mum looked very determined then. 'Becky, I promise you that I'm going to do everything I can to sort this. I'm not going to let him ruin Matt's life again. If Keith's going to play dirty, then, by God, so shall I!'

I'd never heard Mum speak like that. It was really scary. And she's never been much of a drinker, either, but that evening, she had a couple of stiff drinks, and then she was on the phone again. She made the calls from her bedroom, behind the closed door, so I don't know who she was phoning or what she was saying, but I know she would have heard if I'd tried to listen in from the phone in the hall so I didn't even try.

You should have seen her when she'd finished. I'd never believed that eyes could flash, but I do now! I wouldn't have *been surprised to see her pawing the ground and smoke coming out of her nostrils! She was like a tigress protecting her young and I swear, if Keith had suddenly appeared then, she would have torn him limb from limb!*

And I'd have helped her!

It's horrible to think he's so close. Every time I go outside the house, I'm peering down streets, round the back of buildings, jumping at shadows.

He's got under our skins again. It's affecting us all – Mum, me and Matt.

Five grand! I wish I could think of a way of getting the money and paying off Keith so he never comes near us again.

Some hope!

Melbourne, May 1866

It had been a busy few weeks for Amos. He hadn't wasted his time in Melbourne. As soon as he'd secured a passage on a ship bound for England, he'd set about finding buyers for the two properties up at Edwards Reef. It was a good time to sell. Another hotel had just been built there – the Victoria – the mines were yielding well, and in Melbourne speculators were keen to buy up a going concern.

Henry had given Amos money to buy himself some respectable clothes and it was a convincing, smartly turned out young man who dealt with the would-be buyers and sent them up to Edwards Reef to see the properties for themselves.

When it was time for Amos to leave, he was satisfied that he'd done all he could and that it wouldn't be long before Henry would complete a deal. He'd kept Henry informed of everything he was doing and of when he was due to sail.

To his surprise, Henry sent word that Molly had decided to bring Harriet to Melbourne to see him off on the ship: *'They can stay in one of the hotels there for a couple of nights,'* wrote Henry. *'See how it's run. It could be money well spent.'*

Amos was amused at the thought of Harriet in a Melbourne hotel. They were a sight bigger and smarter than the two wooden shacks at Edwards Reef. How she would preen herself! But Henry was wise to send Molly to take a look at the competition. Molly's good sense and shrewd eye would be invaluable when it came to buying a property here themselves. She'd make a good spy!

The night before he was due to sail, Molly and Harriet arrived at his lodgings. He'd taken special care with his appearance that evening, not for them, but because he was seeing a certain young lady later on. A young lady they knew nothing about.

'My my, Amos,' said Molly, patting his hand. 'I hardly recognised you!'

Harriet said nothing, but Amos could see that she was taken aback by his appearance. She'd only ever seen him as a rough fellow in the bush.

'Well, Harriet, what d'you think?' he said, grinning. 'Am I a fine enough city gentleman for you?'

Harriet blushed and gave one of her habitual sniffs. She still hated him and disapproved of him, but even she had to admit that he looked very handsome in his city clothes. She bit back a flippant retort, however, remembering what Molly had said to her: 'He'll be gone a long while, Harriet, and I want you to part on good terms. So please try to be friendly to him for once, dear, and don't rise to his teasing.'

Perhaps he'll drown at sea, thought Harriet. Perhaps he'll stay in England and never come back. This cheered her up and she made a real effort to be civil to him, dreaming that it might be the last time they'd ever meet.

Amos took them around the town and showed them some of the great buildings, the wide streets, the parks, the fine houses, the River Yarra and the throngs of people.

'There's nothing you can't buy here,' he said, speaking to Harriet. 'All the fancy things you could ever want. You could be a real lady of fashion here, Harriet!'

'My, how it's changed,' said Molly quickly, giving Harriet no time to reply with some crushing remark. 'It's only a few years since I visited Melbourne, but I hardly recognise it, there're that many new buildings. And so many people!

'They call it Marvellous Melbourne,' said Amos, 'because it's grown so fast.'

'And to think that there was nothing here thirty years ago!'

Amos nodded. 'It's a good position for trading,' he said thoughtfully. 'Ships come into Port Philip Bay from all over the world now. Old John Batman knew what he was doing when he founded the city here.'

Molly looked at him and smiled. 'You like the city life, don't you Amos?'

Amos grinned. 'I was born and bred in a great city, Molly. Yes, I like city life. It's in my blood.'

'Then you'll fit in well when we come to live here.'

'And so will I,' put in Harriet, quickly.

'Yes, I think you'll be happy here, Harriet,' said Molly. 'I hope you will,' she added more quietly.

The next morning, Amos boarded ship. Molly and Harriet went down with him to the docks and marvelled at the beauty of his ship which sat, elegant and gleaming, in the water. Harriet read out the name: 'SS Aberdeen'. It was a steamship, but rigged as a three-masted scooner so that sails could be hoisted to supplement the steam power.

There was a hive of activity around the ship. Smartly dressed first-class passengers were boarding, with servants and luggage, porters were shouting and gesticulating, the gulls screamed overhead, and the crew were giving directions. Harriet and Molly were allowed on board, briefly, to see where Amos would be living for the next three months.

The SS Aberdeen was newly built, with long beautiful sleek lines. Molly got talking to one of the crew who told them that the ship's poop deck was sixty-two feet long and nine feet high! The middle portion of the deck was a dining area; there were spacious windows to let in light and large mirrors on the walls. The floor was carpeted and the furniture was made of dark heavy wood.

They had a chance to peep into the ladies' saloon also and Harriet gasped. She'd never seen anything so lavish – and this was in a ship! The room was inlaid with rosewood set into arched panels decorated with clusters of carved fruit and flowers. One of the crew told them that there was even a library on board, boasting some four hundred books.

But Amos would not be among the privileged passengers who used these grand rooms.

They descended down to the second deck and finally to the third deck, where he would sleep in an iron berth with the other steerage passengers. To Harriet, it looked cramped and spartan compared to the wonderful accommodation they had glimpsed on the way down, but Amos seemed pleased. He said it was well ventilated and much better appointed and modern than the ship he'd come out on nearly five years ago.

'What will you eat?' asked Molly, always practical.

Amos smiled. 'I'll be well fed, don't you fret. There'll be pigs on board, and chickens and a cow or two for milk. And there's plenty of flour for baking bread.'

'Where do they do the cooking?' asked Harriet.

'In the galley. That's up on the poop deck. They have great ovens there and plenty of fresh water and other supplies.'

'And how many can the ship carry?'

'When I booked my berth, they told me that the ship can take up to one thousand people.'

Molly's eyes widened. 'Why, that's more than all the folk at Edwards Reef put together!'

'Aye,' said Amos. 'A regular floating town! And not only people and food to carry, there'll be tons of coal to keep the boilers going and tons more cargo below – wool and ore and such like.'

At last they had to say goodbye to him and reluctantly they left the ship. On the quay, they waved their kerchiefs at him as he stood at the rail with hundreds of other passengers, but he only gave them a quick salute before his restless eyes went on searching the crowd below.

Harriet followed his gaze and soon saw why he no longer had eyes for them.

Standing a little way off from them, waving to him and blowing kisses, was one of the prettiest young women that Harriet had ever seen. She was fine boned and elegantly dressed, with a grace about her which immediately made Harriet feel gawky and clumsy.

Harriet stared at her. She couldn't be friendly with Amos, could she? Not someone like that? She looked far too well bred!

As she watched the exchange between them, Harriet was suddenly overcome with such a confused jealousy that she had to turn away so that Molly didn't see the hot tears spring to her eyes.

But Molly missed nothing. She had seen the young woman and the look on her face, and she wondered whether that pretty face would still be waiting for Amos when he returned. Then she glanced at her daughter's crumpled face and sighed. She was difficult to understand, was Harriet. She was a complicated one, that was for sure.

The hooter blared out for the last time, smoke belched from the funnel and the ship moved slowly across the great expanse of Port Philip Bay before it slipped through the narrow heads and out into the Southern Ocean.

'Please God, keep him safe,' prayed Molly, as she watched it move away. 'And send him back to his father.'

But Harriet sent up no such prayer. She was thinking of all the shipwrecks there had been on the hazardous journey from Australia to England. Half of her wanted him to drown at sea and never come back. But the other half yearned for him to return.

5

London, August 1866

Amos had enjoyed the voyage. He'd loved the sea and all the strange sights and the changing climate and light. But they'd had their share of storms and sickness and there'd been some terrifying moments. Probably the worst of these was shortly after leaving Melbourne, when they were travelling down the western Victorian coastline. Tremendous gusts of wind hurled gigantic breakers against the rocky ramparts and Amos well imagined why this was known as the 'shipwreck coast'. At the height of the storm, Amos thought of his father and marvelled that he'd escaped when his ship had gone down. If the SS Aberdeen went down, Amos knew that he would never be able to swim through these vast waves to safety.

The vessel pitched and rolled in the heavy seas, but kept its course.

Then, again, in the Indian Ocean, a strong north-easterly gale and high cross seas almost demasted her.

But, despite these frightening times, the Captain had made good progress and, three months after leaving Melbourne, the SS Aberdeen made her way up the River Thames and into the London docks.

It was a muggy summer's day when Amos disembarked. He breathed in the smells of London and the great grey river, so different from those of Melbourne and more different still from the sounds and smells of the bush in Gippsland.

The noise and the crowds were what struck him first. So many people, such a stink. He grinned to himself. He'd missed it.

He'd written from Melbourne to tell Sarah he was coming, but he had no way of knowing whether the letter would reach her before he did. For all he knew, it had come on the SS Aberdeen with him!

He searched the faces at the docks, but there was no sign of Sarah or Abbie or Uncle Edward, so he shouldered his bag and hailed a hansom cab. He decided to go to Edward's workshop first. Sarah would no doubt be at the dress shop and he didn't want to barge in there straight away. He'd always felt awkward among all those girls and flounces and petticoats.

It felt strange to be coming back. And still stranger to arrive in a hansom at Uncle Edward's workshop. He paid off the driver and opened the workshop door.

The smell of leather instantly took him back five

years. As he glanced round, he noticed some changes – a new building out the back, the whole place tidier and better ordered.

A young boy rose from the bench where he was working and came forward. 'Yes sir?'

Amos frowned. The lad was new. And there was no sign of Uncle Edward, or of his cousin James.

'Is Edward not here?' he asked. 'Or James.'

The lad hesitated. 'They're at Mr Edward's house,' he said at last.

'Well, I'll go and find them there, then,' said Amos, smiling.

'Er . . .'

'Well what is it?'

'I dunno as you should go, sir. His wife is very ill.'

Amos stopped in his tracks. 'Abbie? What ails her?'

The boy hung his head. 'She's very sick,' was all he would say.

Amos stood there for a moment, then he made up his mind, and without saying anything to the boy, he turned on his heel and walked the few yards to Edward and Abbie's house.

He walked slowly, gathering his thoughts. If they didn't know he was coming, it would be a shock. If Abbie was very sick, maybe he shouldn't intrude. But then Sarah might be with them. Suddenly he ached to see his mother.

At the door to their house, he hesitated. He put his bag down and knocked gently.

There was no answer, so he knocked again.

A low murmuring came from inside and someone was coming at last.

Amos swallowed nervously and wiped his sweating hands down the side of his breeches.

The door was opened slowly by a very beautiful young woman and for a few seconds Amos couldn't work out who she was. Then he realised.

'Victoria!' he said, smiling broadly.

This beauty was Abbie's daughter. She had been a shy fourteen-year-old when he'd last seen her.

She frowned. 'Yes?'

'D' you not recognise me, Vicky?'

She shook her head.

'It's Amos,' he said. 'Your cousin Amos. Back from Australia.'

She gasped and her hand flew to her mouth. 'Amos! I can't believe it! We thought never to see you again.'

'When I heard about Seth, I had to come and see Mam,' said Amos simply.

Vicky nodded. 'She'll be that pleased, Amos. She's gone out to fetch more medicine, but she'll be back in a while. Come along in with you.'

Amos picked up his bag and walked inside. There was the hushed atmosphere of the sickroom inside.

'What ails your mam, Vicky?'

Vicky's eyes filled with tears. 'She's not got long to live, Amos. They say its consumption.'

She led him through the front room to the bedroom at the back of the house. Amos couldn't help noticing how things had changed. There was more furniture now, some richly coloured drapery, and several plants in china vases sitting on tables which were covered with tasselled cloths.

And there, lying in a large bed, with Uncle Edward sitting at her side, was Aunt Abbie.

In spite of himself, Amos caught his breath. She looked so pale – and so small – and her breathing was very laboured.

Her eyes were closed, so she didn't see him. But Uncle Edward did and he leapt to his feet. At first, thinking that the tall tanned man before him was a total stranger, he looked furious at the intrusion. But then, suddenly his expression changed as he recognised his nephew.

'My God, it's Amos!' Edward said, staring at him and swallowing hard to supress a rush of different emotions. Then, putting his hand gently on Abbie's thin arm, he said. 'Abbie, wake up! 'It's young Amos come back to see us.'

Abbie's eyes opened and slowly she focused on Amos. She stretched out her hand to touch him.

Amos knelt down beside the bed, drew her hand up to his mouth and kissed it. And this time he was not ashamed of the tears that flowed freely down his cheeks.

'God bless you, Amos,' she whispered, the words forced from her wheezing chest.

'Don't try to speak, Aunt Abbie,' said Amos. 'Please don't speak.'

'Sarah will be back any moment,' said Edward. 'She's gone to fetch more medicine; she's bin nursing Abbie night and day.'

'Did she get my letter? When she told me about Seth, I wrote her saying I was coming home.'

Edward shook his head slowly. 'No, lad, she would have said if she'd heard from you.'

Amos continued kneeling by the bed a while, quietly. So much sadness here, with Seth drowning and now Abbie so sick. He'd been worried that he'd not be welcomed by Abbie and Edward, after taking the money and the snuffbox, but bigger tragedies had overwhelmed them and it was obvious his misdemeanours had been long forgotten.

Then there was a noise at the door and Amos jumped up and ran out of the bedroom and into the front room.

The door latch lifted and Sarah came in. For a moment, blinded by the sun outside, she didn't see Amos standing in the shadows and he was able to observe her.

She looked older and very tired. She was no longer the plump and pretty mother that he remembered. She'd lost weight and it didn't suit her. Her face was lined and gaunt.

Amos stepped forward. 'Mam,' he said quietly.

Sarah started and looked into the gloom. She clutched the medicines to her chest. 'Who is it? Who's there?'

'Mam. It's Amos!'

He came towards her slowly, but she didn't move. She just continued to stare at him and the colour drained from her face.

'Are you a ghost?' she whispered.

Amos laughed. 'No ghost, Mam. Just Amos come back from Australia to see you. I got your letter about Seth.'

And then Sarah took in what he was saying. The medicines fell from her hands and rolled over the floor as she lunged towards him and flung her arms round his neck.

'Oh Amos! Amos! And I thought never to see you again.'

He hugged her tight, in a way he'd never been able to as a child. 'I'm so sorry, I'm so sorry,' he kept repeating.

Was he saying sorry about Seth – or was he saying sorry for all the grief he had caused her in the past?

Neither of them knew.

When they had stopped crying and laughing, Sarah shakily gathered up the medicines and took them through to Abbie. But she returned almost immediately and, leading Amos by the hand, she made him sit down and tell her all about his life.

They talked for hours that day, as the afternoon wore on into evening. People came and went through the house, but no one disturbed them. Sarah knew from his letters what he'd been doing, where he'd worked, but she was hungry for every detail. He found himself describing everything: the properties where he'd worked, life as a digger, the harsh life in Gippsland, how he'd met up with Henry Jones and how together they were going to build up the hotel business in Melbourne.

She was so animated, so pleased at his success. And she asked repeatedly about this kind man, Henry Jones, who had helped Amos on his way.

Amos found himself speaking very naturally about Henry, but the more he spoke about him and about Molly and Harriet and his life at Edwards Reef, the more he realised that he could never reveal Henry's true identity to Sarah.

'Fancy, Amos, you doing so well in Australia!'

It was on the tip of his tongue to say that she should come out herself one day, but then he realised that she never could. She would be terrified to make the voyage and she would feel awkward and ill at ease in an unfamiliar place. In any case, it would be impossible because of Henry.

Sarah looked him up and down. 'And what of this young Harriet, Amos? You speak of her a good deal. Are you two courting?'

Amos snorted with laughter. 'No Mam, young Harriet is not for me. She's too stuck up and silly.' And, he added to himself, she's my half-sister.

'You can't tell me there's no young woman in your life,' said Sarah.

Amos smiled. 'Yes,' he said quietly, 'there is someone.'

And then, for the first time, he spoke about the girl at

the docks in Melbourne. He'd spoken to no one about her before, but he told his mother everything and she listened intently.

'It'll not be easy, son, you'll have a fight on your hands, I see that,' she said thoughtfully, 'but it sounds as though you really love her.'

'Yes, Mam, I do. I truly do. In the way that I've never loved anyone before.'

Sarah sighed and pressed his hand. 'Then I wish you all the luck in the world when you go back to her,' she said.

Amos looked at Sarah's eager eyes. Such trust – and he could never tell her the whole truth about his life. But it was better that way.

Briefly he thought of his special girl in Melbourne. She trusted him, too, he was sure of it. He'd told her all about his past and she'd accepted it. But there was one thing he couldn't bring himself to tell her; it would shatter her trust in him and he couldn't bear it if that happened. He'd told no one about it and he prayed that he'd never need to.

At last Amos rose to his feet and stretched. 'Yes, Mam, I'll need all the luck in the world when I go back to her,' he said. 'But I'll spend some time here first. I want to catch up with you and I want to get to know Seth's wife and baby.'

And, although he didn't say so, they both knew that he also wanted to be there to help when Abbie died.

It couldn't be long.

* ★ *

For the next few days, Amos revisited his old haunts and looked up some old friends, and he got to know Seth's gentle wife, Liza, and their baby son.

One day when he went to visit Abbie, Edward told him he needed to see to some business and he asked Amos to sit with his aunt while he went out. So, for the first time, Amos was alone with her.

As soon as Edward left, Abbie became very agitated and Amos thought that she wanted Edward to come back. He reassured her that Edward wouldn't be gone long, but she shook her head and gestured for Amos to come closer so that she could whisper to him.

'Did you find him?' she asked, but her voice was so low that Amos didn't catch the words. He leaned closer. 'Did you find him?' she repeated. Her eyes were full of anxiety.

Amos thought that she was rambling. 'Who, Aunt Abbie?'

She plucked at the bedcovers nervously but her gaze held his. 'Jim.'

For a moment, Amos felt quite numb. His mind raced. How could he tell her the truth? Yet how could he lie to a dying woman? And how could she know that he had gone looking for his father? She thought that Jim had drowned. But had she, like him, always wondered whether he'd escaped the shipwreck and made a new life for himself?

He looked away from those anxious eyes. 'I can't . . .' he began.

And, uncannily, she read his mind. 'You can't tell Sarah?' she got out, eventually, through a bout of coughing.

He shook his head.

'I'm dying, Amos. Tell me the truth.'

Still he said nothing.

'What you tell me will go with me to the grave.'

Amos looked at her and knew that she meant it. Abbie understood the hurt that Sarah had suffered at Jim's hands and she didn't want Sarah to be hurt again – nor did Amos. But Abbie and Jim had been close; maybe Abbie had always suspected that he was still alive.

Amos leant over and whispered in her ear. 'He *is* alive, Aunt Abbie.' He paused. 'He changed his name to Henry Jones.'

Abbie's eyes widened and immediately she understood.

'The man you work for? Who's bin so good to you?'

Amos nodded. 'The very same.'

Abbie squeezed his hand, though there was no strength in the squeeze.

'Thank you, Amos,' she said.

Until Edward returned, Amos told her as much as he knew of Jim's new life in Australia. Of the shipwreck, his escape, his work on properties and how he had built the hotels in Gippsland. And he told her of Molly, too.

He was surprised at how warmly he spoke of Molly,

the woman who had taken his own mother's place. Her gentle acceptance of him had touched him and he had come to love her.

But Harriet was another matter! He tried to find the words to describe her to Abbie without sounding harsh, but his irritation with her came through.

'You're not fond of her?' It was more of a statement than a question.

Amos shook his head.

'Try, Amos. Try, for Jim's sake. And for Molly's.'

Amos looked down at his aunt, lying there, so small and frail, but still with fire in her eyes. He sighed.

'I'll try, Aunt Abbie. I promise.'

And he really meant it.

Then Edward returned and Amos talked of other things. But when he got up to leave, Abbie stroked his face as he bent to kiss her goodbye.

'Thank you, Amos,' she said. 'Thank you so much.'

At the door to the room, Amos turned. Some deep instinct made him take a long, last look at Abbie lying there. She had heard what she wanted to hear and now she could let go. He was quite certain he'd not see her alive again.

When he went into the front room, he walked slowly over to Abbie's desk. He dug deep into the pocket of his breeches, drew out a small package and placed it on the desk.

Edward watched him.

'It's Abbie's snuffbox,' said Amos, hoarsely. 'I've brought it back.'

Edward nodded, then he put an arm around Amos. 'She seems peaceful now,' he said. And then he gave Amos a strange look. 'What did you speak of?'

'About Australia,' said Amos shortly. And then he left quickly before Edward could question him further.

A few days later, Abbie died peacefully in her sleep. They buried her in the same graveyard as her mother.

Edward was desolate without her. He was never one to show his feelings much and he hid them now in a frenzy of work. He pushed himself night and day to get more business and he expected everyone to work as hard as he did.

'He'll put himself in an early grave too,' muttered his son James.

'Can't you make him slow up?' asked Amos.

James shook his head. 'There's no reasoning with him. I tell him that Mam wouldn't want it, but it does no good. He takes no heed of anyone.'

But the person who really surprised them was Sarah. She was no needlewoman – never had been – but she had a talent for getting the best from people. Quietly and tactfully, she made some changes at the dress shop.

Amos watched her emerge from Abbie's shadow and begin to set her own stamp on things.

'You're a good manager, Mam,' he told her one day. 'I

never thought to see you take on so much.'

Sarah smiled. 'It's a grand little business, Amos,' she said. 'And I want to make sure it keeps that way – for Abbie's sake.'

Soon Amos would have to return to Australia. Watching Sarah become so involved with the dress shop, he felt he could leave without hurting her too much. She still grieved for Seth and for Abbie, but she had her little grandson now and Seth's young widow was helping her in the shop. She had her own life and it was a full one.

One evening, when he was alone with her, Sarah said suddenly, 'You'll be leaving soon, Amos?'

Amos was taken aback. He'd been wondering how to tell her and yet, here she was, suggesting it.

He smiled. 'You'll not mind me leaving?'

Sarah shook her head. 'You have a good life over there, Amos. You're making sommat of yourself. I'm that proud of you. And from all you've told me I can see you there, in my mind's eye like.'

'I wish—' began Amos.

'No good wishing, son. You can't be in two places at once!'

Amos grinned. She'd read his thoughts again.

'Besides,' she went on. 'That kind Henry Jones is needing you. And what of the young lady you left behind?'

Amos looked down at his hands. 'I dunno, Mam. It's

bin so long. And I'm the last person her family would want her to wed.'

'Amos, I could shake you sometimes, honest to God, so I could! You're a good-looking young man. You've got a business to build up; you're making sommat of yourself. What does it matter who your father was? It weren't your fault he left us and disappeared to Australia.'

'No,' muttered Amos.

She frowned. 'Did you ever visit the place where 'is ship was wrecked?' she asked suddenly.

'No,' lied Amos. 'Never.'

'You know, I think of 'im sometimes,' said Sarah. 'I wouldn't 'ave wished that end on 'im, whatever he did to us.'

'No,' said Amos, hoping that she'd not see the blush that came to his face.

Then Sarah heaved herself out of her chair. 'Life must go on,' she said. 'And you follow your heart, son. Go after that gel and to hell with her family.'

Amos smiled. 'It'll be a fight, Mam. They'll make trouble, that's for sure.'

'If *she's* worth it, then it's worth the fight,' Sarah replied firmly.

Bedford, present day, February

It was such a shock. I picked up the post from the doormat this morning and sorted it out. Mostly circulars, as usual. But there was one which must have been delivered by hand. It just had Mum's name written on it. I didn't think anything of it at the time, just left it on the kitchen table for Mum to see when she came down.

I was standing, leaning against the cooker, gulping down some cereal from a bowl, when she came into the kitchen.

I can picture it exactly. It's sort of imprinted in my mind.

When I saw her, I thought how good she looked in her business suit. 'Power dressing' she called it! She had got some orange juice from the fridge and she had just turned round after shutting the fridge door when she saw the letter.

She stood there, the carton of juice in her hand, staring at it.

'What's the matter?' I said. And at first, she didn't say anything but just stood there, like a statue.

I'd followed her gaze to the letter. And suddenly I understood. She'd recognised the handwriting.

'Oh my God, it's from him, isn't it? It's from Keith?'

She'd nodded then.

'You'd better open it, Mum,' I said quietly.

She shook her head. 'I don't want to know what it says,' she whispered. 'Tear it up, love and put it in the bin.'

'But Mum,' I said. 'It could be about Matt.'

The mention of Matt's name seemed to trigger something in her head. She went to the table, put the juice down and picked up the letter. She ripped open the envelope and drew out a sheet of paper. I tried to peer over her shoulder but she turned away from me.

'What does it say?'

Mum was shaking; I could see the paper trembling in her hands.

'What does it say, Mum?'

Then she crushed it in her hand and put it in the bin.

'He's mad,' was all she would say.

I had to go to school then and I couldn't get anything more out of her. She just said it wasn't worth bothering about.

But I did bother. I bothered about it all morning. I knew that the rubbish was collected later and that Keith's letter would be chucked away by the time I got back from school.

I told Katie about it, and she agreed to come back to the house with me at morning break. We had a free lesson after break, so, if we hurried, we could just make it there and back in time.

We felt like a couple of burglars, creeping into the house dragging the two back rubbish bags up the path and opening them up in the kitchen. It was disgusting, but I figured that it was the only way I was going to get to know what was going on.

Well, we found the note in the end. A teabag had leaked all over it and it was soggy and crumpled, but we managed to straighten it out and read it.

Then I wished I hadn't. Perhaps Mum was right to chuck it straight in the bin, where it belonged.

This is what it said: 'I'm watching you. I know where

you live. I know where you work. I know where Becky goes to school. Matt owes me £6,000. Get the money.'

He might just as well have said 'or else'.

Katie and I stared at it. I felt sick as we put back all the rubbish into the black bags again. And it wasn't just the smell of the rubbish that made me want to puke.

We managed to get the rubbish bags back outside again just before the truck came up the street to collect them.

Six thousand pounds! How could it be that much? Five thousand was bad enough.

I can just imagine how Keith is enjoying this in his twisted way. He's getting his own back now, and he's going to enjoy scaring Mum.

He's going to stalk her. And me, too. That's what that letter was all about. It's not just the money he wants. He wants to make our lives a misery again.

I put the letter in my pocket. I wondered if I should show it to the police. But then, they'd have to know about Matt owing the money.

It's such a mess.

Katie and I had to leg it to get back to school and, just before I went in, I glanced round. Would he be there, waiting, when I came out? And if he was, what would he do to me?

He wasn't, thank God. Not this afternoon anyway. But he's around; I can sense it.

It's horrible. I can't concentrate on anything and I jump at the slightest sound.

How dare he? How dare he try to ruin our lives again!

6

Melbourne, July 1867

Amos gripped the rail as the ship slid through the narrow heads into Port Philip Bay. He'd not enjoyed the journey much this time. There had been storms and sickness and his fellow passengers in steerage had been poor company. And he was torn, too. Torn between his family in London and his father and his new life here in Australia. In his heart, he knew he'd make his way here in Melbourne better than he ever could in London, but he had hated leaving Sarah and his cousins and his little nephew.

He'd written well ahead this time and he was sure that Henry would be there to meet him. And maybe Molly and Harriet, too.

But would *she* be there? Would she have been able to slip away from her family?

She'd written faithfully, but it had been nearly a year. Had she changed? Had *he* changed? And would her feelings be strong enough to rebel against her family?

All the long way across the bay the thoughts raced round and round in his head. By the time the ship finally docked, his stomach was churning and his heart was beating unnaturally fast.

There were so many people on the dockside, jostling and shouting, that it was hard to see if Henry was there. It was only when Amos stopped trying to find them in the crowd that he spotted his father and Molly, and then Harriet.

He let out a low whistle when he saw Harriet. Even from this distance, he could see how she'd changed. She was fifteen now, going on sixteen. She wasn't a beauty but she was striking, and folk nearby were looking at her with admiration.

'Little Harriet,' he muttered to himself, smiling. 'Well well.'

It took an age to disembark. The crowd seethed beneath the ship, people waving and shouting all the time, but at last Amos was on dry land again, standing firm on Australian soil, his bag slung over his shoulder.

He took a deep breath. This was where he belonged. This was where he would stay.

'Amos!'

He turned quickly. It was Molly, picking up her skirts and running towards him, her arms outstretched. Amos dropped his bag and hugged her in a spontaneous gesture of real affection.

Then Henry was beside him, grinning from ear to ear, and Harriet, too, looking unsure.

'Eh, but we've missed you, Amos,' said Molly.

'I've missed you, too,' said Amos. And it was true. He had.

He turned to look at Harriet. 'My, Harriet, you've grown into a handsome young lady while I've bin gone,' he said.

'Hasn't she just!' said Henry, proudly.

Harriet blushed deeply. Amos went to take her hand, but she turned aside, awkward and embarrassed.

'We've started on the building, lad,' said Henry, as they walked away. 'The hotels in Gippsland sold well and we've found a good site for the new place in Melbourne.'

'Aye, I got your letters. That's grand news,' said Amos, but his eyes were everywhere, scanning faces, looking among the crowd for the one face he really wanted to see above all others.

He was only half listening as Henry droned on about the construction and Molly spoke of materials and furnishings. But he couldn't give it his full concentration; not now. Not until he saw her, spoke to her, heard from her own lips that she hadn't changed her mind.

And then he saw her. She was standing some way off, watching him, shy of interrupting his reunion with his family.

Amos's heart almost stopped beating from excitement.

He dropped his bag and ran towards her, jumping over other people's luggage, squeezing past knotted groups of people.

'Flo!' he yelled.

She smiled and started towards him.

People turned to stare as they met. They made a handsome couple and you could sense the passion between them.

Amos lifted her up off the ground and swung her round, then he held her away from him and just looked at her.

So beautiful and so poised. How could she love such a rough fellow?

He couldn't stop grinning.

'You waited for me,' he gasped, at last.

'Of course I waited,' she said, smiling back at him. 'I love you!'

'You've not changed your mind?'

She shook her head. 'Of course not.'

He held her hand and led her gently back to where Henry, Molly and Harriet stood, uncertainly.

'Molly, Henry, Harriet,' said Amos. 'This is Florence Delaware.'

Flo extended her gloved hand and Henry took it awkwardly, stunned when he heard her name.

'Pleased to meet you, miss,' he said.

Molly, instinctively, bobbed a curtsey. 'Delighted, I'm sure,' she said stiffly.

But Harriet's face was pale and rigid. She said nothing.

Amos was too happy to worry about their reaction. He knew it would be a shock.

Florence was the only daughter of one of the best known businessmen in Victoria. Everyone knew her father, Francis Delaware. He was a friend of the Governor; he moved in exalted circles and was a major benefactor in the city. Francis Delaware had very strong views about who his daughter should marry. The illegitimate son of an ex-convict would certainly not meet his approval.

Francis Delaware knew nothing about Amos. But that was going to change. Somehow Amos was going to overcome all the difficulties in their way and make Flo his wife.

Sarah's words came back to him: 'If *she's* worth it, then it's worth the fight.'

Amos turned to Henry, who was still looking astonished.

'Can we go and look at this new hotel of yours? Now?' he asked.

Henry, recovering himself, nodded. 'I don't see why not. Shall we show 'im, Molly?'

Molly was still looking nervously at Flo.

'Aye,' she said at last. 'You'll be that pleased, Amos. It's a grand site.'

Amos looked down at Flo. 'Come with us,' he said suddenly.

Flo frowned. 'I don't know, Amos. You should be with your family at a time like this.'

'Please! Anyways, you will be my family soon,' replied Amos quietly.

It was spoken so low, that Henry and Molly didn't hear the words, but Harriet's sharp ears had picked them up. Florence Delaware! How could Amos think he'd be worthy of someone like that! He was a rough miner, that's all he was. And a bastard at that. She flushed angrily at the thought.

Florence noticed her discomfort and turned to her. 'That's a pretty bonnet you're wearing, Harriet. It suits your colouring.'

Harriet mumbled something and blushed even more deeply. She wanted to hit out at Flo, tell her she mustn't marry Amos. She was too good for someone rough like him.

But all the while, she refused to admit that the real reason for her anger was jealousy. She was jealous of Flo, jealous of her poise, her confidence, her beautiful clothes and her position in society. And, in her confused way, not even admitted to herself, she was jealous because Flo was loved by Amos.

In some subtle way, Harriet's attitude towards Amos had changed since the day they'd come to see him off and she'd seen him all dolled up in his smart clothes. She'd seen a different Amos that day.

All this time she had waited. Taken special care with

her appearance today. Counted the days until the ship was due in. Hating herself for longing to see him, but being unable to supress her excitement. Thinking that they'd have him to themselves again and that they'd all live a smart city life one day.

And now, this! She had never believed that the pretty girl she'd seen when Amos left was anything more than one of his flirtations.

Harriet fought back the tears. Why was she so jealous? She didn't understand her own emotions.

She trailed behind the party as they walked away from the docks and up to a waiting horse-drawn cab, then she squeezed in last, wedging herself against the side as the horse trotted off and the wheels of the cab lurched over the rutted track which led into the town.

As they made their uncomfortable progress, Flo chatted to Henry and Molly. Harriet, in a fury, observed her. Gradually, Flo was putting them at their ease, asking them about life in Gippsland, about the new hotel and their plans. It wasn't long before they were more relaxed with her, less suspicious of her.

Amos was sitting beside Harriet and she was acutely conscious of his bulk squashing into her. She tried to edge away from him but there was nowhere to go. When he leaned forward and whispered in her ear, she felt the unwelcome blush cover her cheeks again.

'Well, Harriet. What do you think of my Flo?'

Harriet sniffed. 'Very nice, I'm sure.'

Amos laughed. 'She's a deal more than that, Harriet. And just think,' he continued, whispering in her ear again, 'she knows all the grand folk in Melbourne. You'll enjoy meeting them, won't you?'

He was teasing her and she knew it. She'd forgotten how much she hated his teasing.

'Her family won't let you marry her!' she whispered back, viciously.

Amos sighed. 'It won't be easy,' he agreed. Then he looked across at Flo. 'But she's a determined young lady, Harriet. She may yet find a way to bring them round to her way of thinking.' And, he thought to himself, just so long as my secret is safe from her. The one thing I can't tell her.

Harriet sniffed again and peered absently out through the clouds of dust kicked up by the horses and the cab wheels. They were going over the River Yarra and into Flinders Street. They were nearly there.

In spite of herself, Harriet felt a thrill of pride as they got out of the cab. For most of the past year, they'd lived in lodgings near the site while Henry and Molly supervised the building of the hotel. Harriet had watched it grow up from the foundations on a piece of rough land into this small hotel. It was nearly finished now.

'It's your inheritance, Harriet,' Henry had told her. 'Bricks and mortar. Not like the old shacks up in Gippsland, eh?'

Trust Amos to be away while father does all the hard work, she'd thought more than once . . .

She watched Amos closely as he got out of the cab, but he showed nothing but genuine admiration.

'It's grand!' he said, over and over again.

'Your father's worked that 'ard,' said Molly. 'Sometimes he's had no sleep for days and nights, worrying about this and that.'

Amos turned to Molly. 'And I don't doubt you worked yerself into the ground too, Molly!'

'Aye, she did that,' said Henry.

'What do you think, Flo?' said Amos.

'It's lovely,' she said simply. Then she added. 'I've been watching it take shape.'

'You've bin here to see it?' said Amos.

Flo nodded. 'You told me where the site was, didn't you, so I've come down here when I could. It's been exciting, watching it grow.'

Henry pointed down the sloping street. 'See, son, I knew this would be a good site, close to the new railway.'

Molly laughed. ' 'E's forgotten it were you who suggested he build it 'ere!' she said.

'Aye,' said Amos, 'I may have thought about the site, but *you've* done the work, the both of you.' He stretched and yawned. 'But I'm back now to help you.'

Henry immediately began to talk about what needing doing, but Molly broke in, firmly.

'Not today, Henry,' she said firmly. 'Give the poor man a chance to find his feet. He's only just got off the boat. Let's take him to our lodgings.'

'I should go home now,' said Flo, quickly.

Amos took her hand. 'Stay a bit longer,' he said.

She shook her head. 'They'll wonder where I've been.'

'I'll come to your house later then,' said Amos.

Flo looked alarmed. 'To my house! But, Amos, my father will be there . . .'

Amos grinned at her. 'Florence Delaware,' he said. 'I would wed you tomorrow if I could. I don't want to wait a minute longer. So, I'd best get to know this father of yours as soon as possible!'

Henry and Molly looked from one to the other of them. Amos, suddenly so sure of himself. Flo, flustered.

'What's your answer, Flo?' said Amos.

Flo nodded slowly. 'If that's what you want.' Then she whispered to him. 'But I'm frightened, Amos.'

'Don't be frightened,' said Amos, gently. 'It's got to be faced and there's no point putting it off.'

Flo looked up at him with a steady gaze. 'Are you sure, Amos? Are you sure you really want this? And so soon.'

'Certain,' he replied. 'Are you?'

'I want to marry you,' she said. 'I'm sure of that.'

Amos took her hand. 'Then we'll face him together.'

Flo said goodbye to an astonished Henry and Molly, but her eyes lingered on Amos once more before she left.

'I'll tell father about you before you come,' she said simply.

'There's my brave girl,' said Amos. Then he found a cab for her and stood watching after it as it made its dusty way back up the road towards the south east and her house in Toorak.

Briefly, he wondered how she'd managed to slip away from home, unescorted. Not for the first time, he admired her determination and resourcefulness.

Molly was the first to recover. 'My, Amos! My, my, my!' was all she could say.

Henry cleared his throat. 'Well, son, you're full of surprises, I'll grant you that.' And he clapped him on the back.

'She's above your station,' said Harriet crisply.

Amos grinned. He was too happy to let Harriet's jibes annoy him.

'Aye, Harriet. D'you think I don't know that? But I fell in love with Flo, not her family.'

The remark was so genuine that, for once, Harriet couldn't think of a reply. She pursed her lips and looked at the ground.

Amos bent down and picked up one of his bags. 'Come on, then. Take me to these lodgings of yours.'

Henry took another bag. 'It's only a short walk,' he said.

'Once the building's all finished, we'll live in the hotel,' said Molly, picking up her skirts and following behind them.

Harriet said nothing. She was still watching the progress of Flo's cab as it became a mere speck in the distance.

That afternoon, Amos and Henry spent a long time together. Harriet was sure they were planning the future of the hotel, a future from which, no doubt, she'd be excluded. But she was wrong.

Amos was telling Henry all about Abbie and Edward and their children, and about Sarah and Seth's wife and young son.

He'd written to tell Henry of Abbie's death, so it was no surprise, but Henry wept as Amos described it.

'Did you say aught about me, son?'

Amos nodded. 'Only to Aunt Abbie. And only right at the end. She'd guessed. She told me she'd never believed you had drowned.'

Henry nodded, and the tears flowed freely down his cheeks.

'I wish I could've seen 'er again,' he said. 'I 'ad so much to tell 'er.'

'I told her what I could, father. She died 'appy.'

'And did she say aught, d'you think, to Sarah or to Edward?'

'About you being alive?'

Henry nodded.

'No, father, I'm sure of it. That secret went to the grave with her.'

Then he told Henry about Sarah, about the success she was making of the dress shop.

'She's content, father. She's doing well for herself.'

'You didn't tell 'er . . . ?'

Amos shook his head. 'I told 'er a lot about Henry Jones, but I never let on who you were. I never said aught about that.'

Henry nodded. 'No need to upset her,' he said. Then he went on. 'I never meant 'er no ill, son.'

Amos grunted and Henry quickly changed the subject.

'Are you really going up to Delaware's house tonight?'

'Aye. Face the old lion in 'is den.'

'Be careful, son. You're not used to folk like that.'

Amos's eyes were hard. 'I'm not such a bad prospect am I? We're building up a tidy little business here.'

Henry frowned, then he said, slowly, 'But you're not bred to it, Amos. The likes of us don't know 'ow they think. 'Ow they be'ave.'

Amos thumped the table between them and Henry saw, once again, the angry young man who had tracked him down at Edwards Reef.

'I spent years doffing me cap and pulling me forelock to the likes of Lord Fanshaw back in London. But it's different 'ere, father. You know that. The toffs 'ere 'aven't bin bred with a silver spoon in their mouths. Some of 'em came from England to escape the law. Some of 'em 'ave built up their businesses from nothing.'

'But son, if they find out about my past . . .'

'You should 'old yer head up high, father. Look how well you've done for yerself.'

Henry looked down at his hands. 'Aye. But I couldn't 'ave done it without your help, Amos. And with Molly's, too.'

'But you *'ave* done it, father! Yer must start thinking of yerself as a toff, now!'

Henry burst out laughing. 'I'll never do that, son.'

Amos grinned. 'Nor me. But I've gone an' fallen in love with one of 'em, and I'm going to do my best to win 'er, fair or foul.'

That evening, Harriet watched as Amos set off for Toorak.

Toorak. The grand houses and the fancy parties. It was another world. A world Harriet ached to be part of. And to think that rough Amos, with no manners, was going to be invited into one of the grandest houses. Not as a tradesman, but as a suitor for the daughter of the house!

He'll be thrown out, thought Harriet. And serve him right, too. They'll soon see through him.

While Henry and Molly pored over more plans for the hotel, Harriet settled herself in a corner of the room and read a book. But the book could have been upside down, for all it mattered. She didn't read a word and her thoughts kept returning to Amos in Toorak. For the life of her, she couldn't picture the scene. What would the likes of Francis Delaware have to say to Amos?

Meanwhile, Amos was nearly there. The quiet leafy streets of Toorak contrasted strongly with the hustle and bustle of the city block. Amos stopped the hansom at the end of Flo's street and walked the rest of the way to the house. He wanted to gather his thoughts before he presented himself at their front door.

For all his show of confidence, Amos was scared. He'd not had much education compared with the likes of Francis Delaware. His father was a convicted thief who had left London in disgrace without ever marrying his mother. He had none of the social airs and graces.

But he was strong and willing and he had prospects.

And, most importantly, he loved Flo.

But how much should he tell her father? Would it be wise to tell him everything?

And then there was the one secret that he'd never tell and he hoped to God it would never come out. That was the only thing in his past that he would keep to himself; keep it until he died.

The house was in front of him now. Flo had described it to him enough times. There was no mistaking the elegant white columns supporting the wide verandah, decorated with fancy ironwork. Amos knew that much of the iron decoration came out on ships from England, ordered in advance from the foundries there. The house stood in a huge garden and it was two storeys high. Amos had never before seen an Australian home which had two storeys. All the homes he'd ever seen were one-storey and made of timber.

Slowly he approached the front door, although he had a strong instinct to go to the back. Memories of the days when he delivered harnesses and saddles to smart houses in London came back strongly; he'd never have dreamt of going to the front door then.

He was wearing his smartest clothes. The ones Henry had bought for him before he left, so that he could cut an impressive figure with prospective buyers of the Gippsland properties. Amos tugged at the jacket. He'd broadened out since then and the jacket was too tight.

He swallowed, cleared his throat and raised the huge metal knocker, bringing it down with a resounding thump on the wooden door.

Almost immediately, there was the sound of light footsteps inside and Amos grinned widely, expecting Flo to appear at the door. But a young maid opened it, neatly dressed in a black uniform with a white pinafore.

For a moment, Amos was stunned into silence. He should have expected it, of course he should, but his mind flew back to his mother's life in London. Sarah would have opened the door at the Fanshaw's. She would have let in the smart visitors at the front door. Or maybe not, maybe she was too lowly. Perhaps she only opened the back door.

The maid looked at him, waiting for him to speak. To Amos, even she seemed to have a superior air.

'I've come to see Mr Delaware,' said Amos, at last, his voice not sounding as strong as usual. To his annoyance, he was sweating with nerves.

'Come in, sir, and wait in the hall,' said the maid.

Amos stood awkwardly in the great entrance hall. It was cool and airy, with a marble floor and some fancy pictures on the walls.

Where was Flo? Why wasn't she here to greet him? To support him?

Angrily, he had to acknowledge that Henry had been right. He was out of place here. It was a way of life he simply didn't understand.

But he loved Flo. He must hold onto that.

The maid returned. 'Mr Delaware's expecting you,' she said. 'Come this way.'

She led Amos along a passage. In the distance, Amos could hear a piano being played. He smiled suddenly. It must be Flo. She was playing the tune they'd danced to, when they'd first met, when, just for devilment, he'd sneaked into some smart Assembly Rooms and found a society dance going on. And then he'd seen her across the room and she'd agreed to dance with him, though he'd never danced before in his life . . .

'In here, sir,' said the maid, interrupting his thoughts. She opened a great wooden door. 'Mr Delaware's in the library.'

Amos walked into the room. It was completely lined with books, floor to ceiling, and furnished with a heavy desk and big heavy chairs.

Francis Delaware was standing at the end of the room, staring out of a huge window which overlooked the garden. He turned as Amos entered and Amos saw a well-built, imposing man, with bushy eyebrows and an impassive face. His whole stance gave off a sense of power and self-confidence. He seemed neither welcoming nor threatening and, for a moment, he said nothing, but just looked at Amos. Then he put out his hand and Amos shook it, wishing that his own palms weren't so moist and warm.

'Sit down, young man,' said Francis Delaware.

Awkwardly, Amos perched in one of the large chairs. And Francis Delaware sat opposite him, observing him.

'I've come—' began Amos.

Francis Delaware cut him short. 'I know why you've come,' he said shortly. Florence has told me all about you.'

Amos smiled. Perhaps this wasn't going to be so hard, after all.

'I love her, sir,' he said. 'And we want to get wed.'

'And you've come to seek my permission?'

Amos nodded. 'Yes.'

'Then you'd better tell me about yourself.'

Amos suddenly felt more relaxed. He wouldn't lie to this man. He would tell him everything about his past life. Well, everything except that one secret. So he began to speak. He told him about his father's wrongful conviction, about Seth and Sarah and his upbringing and about his voyage to Australia and his quest to find his father. He told him about the mining and the hotels in Gippsland and about the new hotel they were building.

The big clock in the library had moved on almost an hour before he stopped talking.

'That's all there is, sir,' said Amos. 'That's my life up till now.'

Francis Delaware stood up and stretched. He walked to the window and back again, without saying anything. Then he stopped beside Amos.

'I admire you, young man,' he said.

Amos felt a surge of joy going through him. This would be all right. Flo's father would give his permission!

'I admire your honesty,' continued Francis Delaware. 'And you are obviously a hard worker. Both very commendable traits.'

'I'd make her happy, sir. I promise.'

Francis looked at him. 'No, Amos,' he said firmly. 'You would not make her happy.'

Amos looked shocked. 'We love each other! We want to spend our lives together.'

Francis shook his head. 'I've no doubt you think you love each other,' he said. 'And no doubt you'd be happy for a while, Amos, but you come from different worlds.

Florence wouldn't fit into your life and you'd not fit into hers.'

Amos sprang to his feet. 'Please, sir. I love her!'

Francis nodded. 'She's very loveable, and she's headstrong, too, Amos. But I fear she's not for you.'

'Have you told her this?'

Francis shook his head. 'I promised her that I would see you, that I would hear you out. That's all I said to her.'

'But—'

Francis Delaware held up his hand. 'There's no more to be said. Let me escort you to the door.'

Amos stumbled after Flo's father, unable to comprehend the finality of the dismissal. How could this man, with just a few terse words, ruin the future happiness of two people who loved each other so much?

As they came out of the library, Amos could hear the piano still tinkling away in the distance. But as the library door shut behind them, the piano also stopped abruptly and a moment later, Flo was running down the stairs into the hall to greet them.

'Well?' she said to her father.

He put his arm round her shoulders. 'I told you to stay upstairs,' was all he would say.

'Can we marry, Papa?'

He said nothing, so she looked at Amos and immediately saw the answer. She rushed to him and held his face in his hands.

'We *shall* marry, Father — whatever you say.'

It was then that Amos saw a man who was not used to being crossed.

'How *dare* you question me, Florence! Go to your room at once.'

But Flo stood there, white-faced.

'Go, or I won't answer for the consequences!'

She turned then and fled upstairs. But at the top she stopped and looked down at Amos. Then she burst into tears and ran along the landing and out of sight.

Amos made to run after her, but Francis moved swiftly to the foot of the stairs, blocking his way.

'Leave this house immediately, young man. And I forbid you to come here again or to see my daughter again.'

'But—'

'GO!'

His mind in turmoil, Amos walked down through the garden and into the street. But he went no further. He would not leave it like this. It broke his heart to see his Flo so miserable.

He turned the corner, well out of sight of the house, and settled down to wait until dark.

He sat on a low wall and sunk his head in his hands. Was it really only a few hours ago that he had got off the boat, so full of excitement, with everything to live for, to look forward to? And now here he was, weary and defeated with his heart in his boots.

The sun sank beneath the horizon and still he waited and watched. He could see movement in some of the other large houses, servants putting out lamps, locking doors, settling horses in stables.

But still he waited.

At last, he rose stiffly, stretched and walked back towards the Delaware's house. Very quietly he crept round to the back and hid behind an outhouse, watching. There was no movement, but there was one lamp still burning in an upstairs room. He stared at it, hoping that he would be able to see someone inside, so he'd know if it was Flo. But there was no sign of anyone.

His heart pounding, he picked up a small stone and threw it at the window. He missed the first time and the stone landed on the wall just below. Its noise sounded shattering to Amos, and he melted back into his hiding place. But no one stirred.

He tried again, aiming more carefully this time, and the stone hit its target. Inside the room, he saw the light moving across to the window. Someone had heard and was walking over to the window to investigate.

Who was it?

Flattened against the wall, hidden from view, he watched as someone opened the window and looked out.

It *was* her!

Amos ran as quickly as he dared, until he was underneath the window. Until he could see her frightened face lit by the lamp in her hand.

'Flo!' he called out. But very softly.

At last she saw him. And immediately she leant forward. 'Stay there, Amos,' she whispered. 'I'll come out to you.'

Amos waited for what seemed an age. He saw that she had turned out the lamp. She must be creeping down the stairs in the dark, trying not to wake her parents or the servants. Creeping down the long passage to the back door. Undoing the bolts.

He held his breath, willing her not to be caught.

He moved slowly and quietly round to the back door. Then there was the slightest scraping sound of the bolts being drawn back, and she slipped out, still in her night things.

He took her in his arms and held her. She was shivering like a frightened animal and sobbing. He stroked her hair.

'Don't cry, Flo, please don't cry!'

'Oh Amos, what shall we do?'

Amos tried to sound firm, but, in truth, he didn't know himself what they could do. All the time, sitting on the wall, waiting for darkness to fall, he'd been trying to find the answer.

'Do you still want me, Flo?' he managed at last.

She sniffed and raised his face to his. 'More than ever,' she said firmly.

'Then, somehow we'll find a way to wed.'

'But my father? He'll be watching me all the time. He

said as much after you'd left. He was so angry, Amos. He has forbidden me to leave the house alone. I must only go out with my mother or a servant.'

'What of your mother? What does she say?'

Flo smiled in the darkness. 'She's a gentle soul, Amos. She's unhappy for me, but she'd never go against my father's wishes.'

'But you would?'

She nodded. 'I'm like him, Amos. I'm strong like him and if I want something badly enough, I fight for it.'

'Then somehow, we'll find a way, Flo,' he said again. 'But we must be patient. We'll have to make our plans carefully.'

They whispered together for a long time, working out a way of keeping contact with each other.

'I must go, Amos,' said Flo, at last.

'Be very careful.'

He came with her to the door.

She slipped inside and turned to give him one last kiss. 'You know he'll make trouble for you, if we do wed in secret?'

'I know that, Flo.'

'And he'll cut me off without a penny.'

Amos smiled. 'I don't want your money, Flo. I intend to make my own!'

He heard the bolts slide into place and he crept round the house again and stood beneath her window until he saw the lamp shine softly inside her room again.

He breathed a sigh of relief. She'd not been discovered. And he must make sure that he wasn't either.

Quietly, he made his way out into the street again. It was very late now, and there was no one around.

It was a long way back to the lodgings, but he welcomed the walk. He needed the time to think. Whatever happened, they must raise no suspicions.

He knew what he'd say to Henry and Molly; that Flo's father had refused to give his permission. They'd be genuinely sad for him and question if there wasn't some way, if he was patient and made something out of the hotel. He'd say that it was final, that it was impossible and that he must forget Flo and throw himself into work.

And Harriet! Harriet would gloat. Tell him, no doubt, again and again, how foolish he'd been ever to think he might be good enough for the likes of the Delawares! Well, he must just grit his teeth and endure her insults. She, above all, mustn't suspect anything.

When at last he let himself into the lodgings, the dawn was breaking and the city was waking. Amos went to his bed and, though he was exhausted through and through, it was still a long time before sleep overtook him.

The next day, Molly was firm. 'You're to stay in and rest, Amos,' she said, after she'd heard about Francis Delaware's refusal. 'You're tired and unhappy. You need some proper rest.'

But Henry was anxious to talk with him about the hotel. 'He'd be better working,' he said to Molly, when they were alone. 'It would take 'is mind off the whole sorry business.'

'Just let 'im be for today, Henry. Let 'im lick 'is wounds in peace.'

'Damn toff!' said Henry, banging his hand down on a handy table. 'It's clear as day that they love each other. He should be proud 'is daughter's got a suitor like Amos.'

Molly sighed. 'It's another world, Henry. You know it.'

Henry nodded. 'Aye,' he said shortly, but still he fumed inside and felt hurt on behalf of his son.

But in a few days' time, Amos seemed more cheerful. He started picking up the threads of his life again, helping Henry with plans, making contacts, overseeing the last of the building works.

Harriet had been unusually quiet when she heard about the Delaware business. Normally ready to jump in with a spiteful remark where Amos was concerned, she'd kept her peace and Amos was surprised and grateful. She'd even offered to come with him when he visited business contacts, but Amos discouraged this. Some of the meetings he'd told them about never existed. They were a cover for his trips to Toorak to drop a note in the secret place that he and Flo had arranged. It was a clever idea. There was a big old gum tree one side of the gates leading up the drive to Flo's house and it had a slit at the back just big enough so that a note could be pushed in and concealed. Amos could reach it without ever going inside the property and Flo could reach it without going outside the property.

As long as they were very careful and made sure that no one saw them putting notes in and out, they were safe, but, even so, they kept the notes to the minimum.

Their plans were taking shape, but they had to be patient.

Bedford, present day, March

Mum's at the end of her tether. She keeps seeing Keith lurking near where she works, in shops in town, even at the end of our street. He's playing some sort of mind game. He never actually fronts up to her, just lets her know he's around.

I told her to go to the police, but she says there's nothing they could do. Keith hasn't touched her. He has every right to be around her workplace or in our street. She says she's got no evidence that he harrassing her.

He's clever. He knows she's getting really scared.

She's been talking to her lawyer friend, too, but Keith's inside the law, apparently.

The bastard.

I keep thinking about the note he sent Mum. I never told

Mum I rescued it from the rubbish. I'm glad I did. That's the only evidence we have that he's threatening her.

And there've been some anonymous phone calls, too. He doesn't say anything, but we know it's Keith on the other end.

Until today. Matt hadn't been in touch for weeks. Then he phoned me on my mobile when I was on my way back from school. He sounded a bit better.

'Becky, can you do me a favour?'

'Sure,' I said. 'Anything.'

Then he explained. Some guy in the music business had seen their website and he'd heard their first CD. He'd sent an email to the band's address and said he wanted to hear them play live. But, of course, just now, they weren't performing anywhere because Keith and his heavies were threatening to come and take away all their equipment. If they advertised any gigs. Keith would hear about it and send his men round. Somehow, Matt had got to find a place to do a gig with an audience but without advertising it.

I had a brainwave then. 'It's Katie's seventeenth birthday soon, Matt, and she's thinking of hiring a hall somewhere. I don't think she's fixed up the music.'

'But we need to do it soon, Becky.'

I thought fast. 'Look I'll talk to her now. See if we can fix something.'

'She won't tell anyone, will she?'

'No. She's the one person who knows everything, Matt. She'll keep quiet, I promise.'

'Ok, that's great. I'll phone you again tonight.'

He was about to hang up, but I stopped him. 'Don't go, Matt. Just tell me what's happening. I want to know, for Mum's sake.'

There was a bit of a silence, then a sigh. 'Yeah. Well, I suppose I owe you that.'

'So?'

'I'm living with friends, Becky. Sleeping on their floor. They're being really good to me and, so far, Keith's not found me, but I've been really careful. I've not been to see other members of the band; we just keep in touch by phone. We're all lying low. But I promise you, somehow, we're going to find the money to pay off Keith, Becky. It would cost a fortune to get all that gear up and running again. He's told us that he's going to seize everything – not just the stuff we bought with the money he lent us, but everything else, too. Everything the band owns.'

We talked for a while about Keith and then I told Matt about him stalking Mum. Perhaps I shouldn't have. He went ballistic.

'We've got to get him off her back, Becky. It's not fair. I got myself into this mess. I've got to get out of it.'

'We'll do it, Matt. We'll find somewhere for you to perform so this guy can come and hear you, then maybe he'll offer you a contract or something.'

Matt laughed then. 'Don't build up your hopes, Becky.'

'He might,' I said.

Then Matt mentioned his name. Even I had heard of him. I was dead impressed.

'Matt, that's fantastic! If he likes you, you're made!'

'He may not like us, Becky. But I've got to give it a go. I've got to let him hear the band. You understand that, don't you?'

'Sure.'

After he hung up, I got straight on to Katie. I didn't say anything over the phone. I'm getting paranoid. I know Keith couldn't tap into my mobile, for heaven's sake, or overhear my conversation, but I feel he's hovering everywhere, always around us. So I just said to Katie that I'd got something I wanted to talk to her about face to face.

She's coming over later.

If anyone can fix it, she and I can!

7

Melbourne, September 1867

The hotel was nearly finished. They were all working as hard as they could. Henry and Amos on the last of the building and on setting up people to work in the hotel, and Molly and Harriet on furnishing the rooms and equipping the kitchen.

Harriet had changed a lot since the Delaware business and seemed a good deal happier. She'd suddenly thrown herself into the work and had been a real help to Molly. She had a good eye for fabrics and fittings and Molly was astonished at how high class the hotel was looking.

Amos approved. 'Well, Harriet, I can see your eye in this,' he said, when she and Molly brought him along to inspect the dining room, which was finally ready. 'It's a far cry from those timber shacks in Gippsland, full of squabbling miners fighting and drinking themselves into oblivion.'

Harriet smiled. 'I'm glad you like it,' she said.

Amos nodded. 'You've both done a wonderful job,' he

said. And he meant it. This little hotel would be a gem.

In mid-September, they moved in. They had rooms at the back on the second floor. They weren't big but they were comfortable and separate from the guests' rooms.

'We've done it, Amos,' said Henry one evening, as they walked round the building together, inspecting every nook and cranny, checking and rechecking.

Two days later the cook arrived and then the rest of the staff they had hired. Molly was to work with the cook and Harriet would help on the front desk, greeting people when they arrived.

'They'll be pleased to see a pretty girl when they walk in through those doors,' said Amos.

Harriet blushed, but she didn't snap back.

Amos had been so busy with the hotel and with his secret plans that he'd not really noticed the change in Harriet before, but when the tart remark didn't come, he looked at her properly and saw a different girl. Striking, for sure, but softer, too, somehow.

He shrugged, inwardly. She was a strange confused creature, this half-sister of his. There was no understanding her and he had no idea what had brought about this change of mood, but he was certainly grateful for it. It made things easier for them all.

She seemed to be more comfortable in his company but he also felt that she was watching him, following his every move.

He must be very careful and cover his tracks. It would

never do if Harriet suspected that he and Flo were still in contact. She could be a danger to him if she did, and nothing must upset his plans – especially now, now that they were almost in place. The hotel was to open in two days' time. He must speak to Henry and Molly soon.

The next day, he found them in their room, making some final checks on a long list.

'I'd like to go away for a few days,' he said.

Henry looked alarmed. 'Not now, son. Not when we're opening!'

Amos laughed. 'No, don't worry, I'll not run out on you now, but I'd like to get away for a few days before Christmas comes.'

'Aye, it'll be that busy over Christmas,' said Molly.

'We hope it will,' said Henry cautiously.

Molly patted him on the hand. 'Don't be so gloomy,' she said. 'We've already had enquiries. It'll be hard work, but we'll get some good custom, you'll see.'

'Aye, mebbe.'

'Of course you will,' said Amos. 'And I'll be there to make sure it goes well, I promise. But before then I'd like to take the steamer up to Sydney.'

'*To Sydney*!' gasped Molly.

'It's not so far, Molly. I'll not be gone long.'

'When would you want to go?' asked Henry.

'The end of next month,' said Amos promptly. 'The end of October.'

'Well . . .'

'Of course 'e must go, Henry,' Molly said quickly. 'The poor man's been working non-stop since 'e got off the boat. He deserves some time to himself.'

Henry nodded. 'She's right, son. You go off and enjoy yourself.'

'Do you know folk in Sydney?' asked Molly. 'Will you be visiting someone?'

For a second, Amos hesitated, but then the lie came easily. 'A fellow I met on the boat coming back from England,' he said easily. ' 'E's asked me to visit. And,' he added, 'I've a mind to spy on some of the hotels they have there, too.'

The opening of the hotel went better than they could have hoped. People poured through the doors, although most of them, as Molly commented, only came to gawp.

'Let 'em gawp then,' said Amos. 'If they like what they see, they'll be back.'

Amos had to work hard on Harriet. She smiled politely enough when the folk were quality, but there were some rough men who came to visit, too, and who wanted to flirt with the pretty girl at the desk.

'I can't abide it,' sobbed Harriet, when Amos found her one evening, having fled from the hotel lobby to hide upstairs.

'It's part of the job, Harriet,' he said firmly. 'Don't take it to heart, so. They don't mean no 'arm. You must learn to go along with it.'

'I can't, Amos, I hate it.'

Amos put his hand under her chin and made her look up at him.

'Now see 'ere, Harriet,' he said firmly. 'If you can't do this job, then we'll 'ave to find someone who can. We can't 'ave you upsetting the customers. Don't you understand that?'

'But they *flirt* with me,' gulped Harriet.

Amos smiled. 'They flirt with you because you're young and good-looking, Harriet. What's the 'arm in that?'

'But—'

'No buts, Harriet. It's part of the job. Now you smile at them all and be polite to them all.'

Harriet hung her head and Amos felt quite sorry for her.

'For me, Harriet, please? Do it for me.' And then, instinctively, he put his arm round her shoulders and drew her to him in a brotherly hug.

When she clung to him, still sniffing, a thought suddenly struck him. Harriet trusted him now. Her whole attitude towards him had undergone some subtle change since the business with Francis Delaware. Did she expect him always to be around to protect her? How would she react when she discovered his plans?

For the world he didn't want to hurt her, but he knew, deep down, that he would soon lose her trust again, probably for ever. Molly and Henry would understand why he'd had to keep everything secret, but Harriet would feel that he'd made a fool of her.

He sighed. That was her nature and there was nothing he could do about it.

Gently, he released her. 'Will you try, Harriet?' he said. 'You're the first person they see when they come through those doors. It's really important they see a friendly face.'

'I'll try,' she whispered.

'Good girl.'

Quickly, Amos turned and left her room.

As he walked down the stairs, he wondered if Henry and Molly had told Harriet that he was going away. He'd best tell her soon, get her used to the idea.

She wouldn't suspect anything would she? He frowned. She picked up on any atmosphere so quickly so he'd have to tell his lies well!

He found a chance to slip it into the conversation later that day. He'd just witnessed Harriet dealing politely but firmly with an awkward customer, so he walked over to the front desk.

'Well done,' he whispered. 'That were capital. Just the right way to 'andle a roughneck like him!'

Harriet looked pleased.

'Just keep that up when I'm away, won't you?'

Harriet looked up, shocked.

'You're not going away again?'

'Didn't Henry and Molly tell you?'

She shook her head.

'At the end of October. I'm going to Sydney to visit a friend I met on the boat coming back.'

'Oh,' said Harriet, flatly.

'Not for long.'

'Who's the friend?'

Amos had rehearsed the answer. 'Oh, 'e's a bloke from London. Called Jonas. 'Is brother came to live 'ere and 'e's come to join 'im.'

Harriet nodded and seemed to take no further interest. Amos strolled away, secretly relieved he'd told her in such a casual way.

But in the days to come, Harriet kept questioning him about this Jonas man. Amos had to invent a whole story surrounding him. And sometimes he wondered whether he'd trip himself up with his lies!

Fortunately, they were all kept so busy that there wasn't much time for chat among themselves.

People came out of curiosity at first but they soon came back because of the friendly atmosphere, the good plain food and the comfort.

One evening, Harriet came to find Amos. She looked very agitated and she took his arm and dragged him away from what he was doing.

'Francis Delaware's here!' she whispered. 'He's having dinner with a group of other men.'

Amos thought fast. He didn't want to make a fuss, just when his own plans were laid. There'd be plenty of fuss to come from Francis Delaware later. But he wasn't going to avoid him, either.

'What are you going to do?' asked Harriet.

Amos hesitated. 'No point avoiding him, Harriet,' he said quietly. 'I'll go and enquire if the gentlemen are enjoying their dinner, just as I always do.'

Harriet looked at him admiringly. 'You're brave, Amos. I'll say that for you.'

If only she knew, thought Amos. Not brave so much as foolhardy.

He straightened his jacket and walked into the dining room, looking at it with pride. It was clean and bright and the food, under Molly's supervision, was always good. Plain, but good. It seemed to be what the customers wanted.

He had nothing to be ashamed of.

He walked up to the group of men – all prosperous and some a little the worse for drink. Francis Delaware looked up as he approached, but he showed no sign of recognition.

'Good evening, gentlemen,' said Amos. 'I hope you are enjoying your meal.'

There were murmurs of 'very good . . . excellent . . . come again.' Very much the same reaction he usually got.

Francis Delaware said nothing but, just after Amos left the table, he noticed that Delaware had leant forward and said something to the rest of the company.

Suddenly there was a gust of loud raucous laughter.

Amos knew, instinctively, that the other men had been told of his cheek in asking for Flo's hand.

Amos kept walking, hoping that the fury he felt inside wouldn't betray him.

Harriet, ever sharp-eyed, had noticed the incident. 'Don't worry yourself Amos,' she said. 'He's not worth it.'

Amos smiled at her gratefully. 'You're right, Harriet. He's not.'

But inside, he was thinking: just a few more weeks, Francis Delaware, just a few more weeks.

Bedford, present day, March

Well, Katie and I have fixed it! At least I hope we have. She was going to have her party in the holidays, but she's persuaded her mum that it's better to have it in term time when everyone's still around, so it's on for next week.

They've hired this hall that's often used for parties and Katie's told her mum that some friends from school will do the music for nothing. Her mum was a bit iffy about it, but then I chipped in and said I'd heard them and they were really cool and that they wouldn't use a lot of bass and disturb the neighbours. All the stuff that parents want to hear.

So, in the end, Katie's parents agreed. The date was difficult, too. It had to be on this particular Saturday, which was the only time the music guy could come down here and listen to the band. At first, Katie's mum said no, not that Saturday, because she had other plans. But, anyway, in the end, with lots of begging and promising and all that, it's settled.

Phew! It's been like an army exercise. Matt phoning me, secretly. Me phoning Katie, secretly. Mum wondering why I'm taking such an interest in Katie's party. Katie asking people to a party without saying what music she's having. Lots of people have asked her but she's been great. Just said it's a new band no one's heard of and that she's giving them a chance to play a gig.

God! I hope this music bloke turns up after all this effort.

And I've got to think of a way of getting Mum to come, too. But with Keith following her all the time, it could be tricky. I'll have to work on that.

Yesterday, I went up in our attic again and dug out the stuff we'd found in the old box, when we moved house — the box from Great Gran.

I sat up there and looked at the gold watch and the snuffbox again. If we can't get the money any other way, maybe we could sell them and pay off Keith like that.

I know they wouldn't be worth six thousand pounds, but I guess if I took them to someone who knew about old things, I could get quite a bit for them. It would all help.

Let's hope it won't come to that. It would be a pity to get rid of them. One day, I must ask Gran about them and find out where they came from.

Melbourne, October 1867

Amos was getting tense as the end of the month approached. He tried not to let it show, but he knew he was being difficult to work with. His mind was on other things, after all. He was about to cross one of the most powerful men in Melbourne. He knew, only too well, that Francis Delaware could make trouble for him in all sorts of ways, including advising his rich friends to boycot the hotel.

He couldn't bear it if all that he and Henry and Molly had built up so carefully was destroyed. In dark moments, he wondered if he was doing the right thing, but then he thought of Flo, of her certainty, her faithfulness and her trust. He didn't fully deserve her trust because he had kept back that one secret from her, but that was because he was so frightened of hurting her. Sometimes he wished he'd told her that even, so that they could start with a clean slate. But it wasn't something he could put in one of the scribbled notes he'd written her. If he ever confessed, then it would have to be face to face.

She was his rock; and she was taking a much bigger risk than he.

Carefully he put his things together for the journey. Secretly he booked their train tickets. They weren't heading up to Sydney, as he'd said, but in the opposite direction, to Geelong. They reckoned this would buy them some time, while Francis Delaware chased after them in Sydney.

Amos made another visit, secretly, to a business contact who owed him a favour. The man was discreet and he arranged for a pastor to marry Amos and Flo secretly, before they set off on the train from Spencer Street. It would happen in the very early morning, before anyone much had stirred and before the train left.

It was all set up. Flo knew what she was to do, where she was to be. Amos had bought for her everything she would need for the journey so she would come with no luggage. Just so long as she could creep out of the house undetected then Amos would pick her up at the end of her street and drive her to the pastor's house.

The official papers were all ready. All the plans had been laid. Amos prayed that no one involved had breathed a word. He didn't think they would, but everything depended on secrecy.

The night before the journey he didn't sleep at all. He was up and ready to go long before the due time. He paced up and down in his room, going over and over every detail and he was wrestling with his conscience, too. Not about deceiving Henry, Molly and Harriet, but about deceiving Flo and not telling her that last damning secret about himself.

But he couldn't tell her. Not now. Some day perhaps, but not now.

At last, he shouldered the two bulging bags, crept

down to the hotel lobby and let himself out of the side door.

He looked anxiously behind him as he walked up the road, but no one followed him. The city was eerily quiet. It was even too early for the milk drays and the mail cart, and any late-night revellers had long gone home to bed.

He saw the hansom waiting for him and quickened his pace. Good! The man was there on time – yawning and stretching, with a half-awake horse between the shafts, but he was there. So he should be, thought Amos, remembering the money he'd agreed to pay him.

Amos nodded to the driver and swung the bags into the cab, then he climbed in himself and they set off, the horse's hooves echoing in the early morning stillness. Usually, Amos would have chatted to the cabbie, but it was too early for small talk and he was too tense.

It seemed an age before they reached Toorak. The sun was creeping up and every moment, Amos expected someone to challenge him. At the hotel, they knew he was going to leave early and he'd said his goodbyes last night. No one would think it strange that he'd left. But as soon as Flo was found missing, there would be a hue and cry, to be sure.

The cab stopped at the end of her street and Amos jumped down. For a moment, he despaired. There was no sign of her! What had happened.

And then he felt a gentle tug at his sleeve and she was there, smiling up at him.

'You didn't think I was going to stand in full view, you silly goose!'

Amos held her close and the tears welled up. 'Flo!' was all he could say.

'Come on,' she said. 'We can't waste a moment.'

He helped her up into the cab and they set off back towards the city.

A few more people were up and about when they headed back, but no one gave the hansom a second glance. They jolted on past the park to a small, elegant house on the other side.

Amos instructed the cabbie to wait for them and he and Flo went inside.

Flo squeezed his arm. 'I can't believe it's really happening,' she whispered.

'Are you sure, Flo? Are you sure you want to marry me? You know how much trouble it will cause.'

'Quite sure, Amos. You know that.'

He kissed her lightly, and then introduced her to the pastor and the two witnesses.

It was a simple ceremony but, for Amos, it was all he'd ever dreamed of. The early morning sun streamed through the windows onto the wooden floor. Flo had taken off her bonnet and stood beside him in her plain travelling dress. She made her vows with an unwavering voice, looking at Amos throughout. As Amos slipped the ring onto Flo's slim finger, his heart was so full that he thought it would burst. And when the pastor announced

'I now pronounce you man and wife,' he could no longer contain his tears.

Flo held his arm very tight. 'Mrs Harris,' she said, smiling. 'I like the sound of it.'

But there was no time to lose. They signed the papers, Amos wrung the hand of the pastor and the two witnesses, and they jumped back into the cab and rattled away to Spencer Street railway station.

Instinctively, as they passed the hotel, they both looked across at it.

'That'll be your home from now on, Mrs Harris,' said Amos.

'It's lovely,' said Flo. And indeed, sitting there, the sun shining on the soft stone, it looked solid and comforting.

'Nearly there,' said Amos, as they stopped outside the station. The cabbie helped them with their luggage and they reached the platform just as the whistle was blowing.

They scrambled on board the train heading for Geelong seconds before it chugged out of the station.

Bedford, present day, March

Tonight was amazing! I'm on such a high that I had to write it down. I can't sleep I'm so excited.

We staked everything on the party, but it was worth it.

Matt said they'd have to hire a van to bring all the stuff down, but of course, no one would hire it to them, they're all too young. And anyway, they are all flat broke.

Crisis number one. I thought the whole thing was going to crash round our ears.

So, at that point, I had to tell Mum what we were doing. She was amazing. I've never seen her so determined. She hired a van herself, from someone in London. Then she hopped on a train and went up to collect it. She even drove to Tesco's first and left the car in the car park, went into the store and called a cab to get to the station. This was a cunning plan to put Keith off the scent.

Then there were more furtive phone calls to me, to Mum, to Matt, about picking up all the equipment.

Poor Mum. She's not a confident driver at the best of times and she hates driving in London. But she did it. She picked up each member of the band, each at a different place and each with a different piece of gear. And they got there, well in time to rehearse.

She even disguised herself when she got near Bedford. She put on a wig and some specs so Keith wouldn't recognise her if, by any remote chance, he saw her.

We'd done this great scam in the morning, too. I'd had this brilliant idea to put Keith off the scent. It had to be subtle or he'd suspect something.

I'd done a poster on the computer about a school play happening in the evening and put it in our front window. We reckoned that, if Keith was nosing round the house, he might see it and then go and hang around the school to get a glimpse of Mum.

Meanwhile, she'd be wearing the wig and specs, driving the van to the hall we'd hired at the other end of town.

Brilliant or what!

Anyway, it worked. She phoned me whan they arrived and I went to meet them, getting on the wrong bus at first to confuse Keith – if he was following me – then doubling back. It took ages, but I was terrified I might blow it for them.

When I got there Matt was looking dead nervous, but even he had to see the funny side of it. Me shaking off the sleuth and Mum wearing a wig!

By that time, they'd already unloaded and got themselves and their gear inside. They didn't want to hang around in full view for any longer than necessary.

I stayed while they rehearsed. Mum and I had made a huge picnic for them so they didn't need to move out of the hall. It was quite scary in one way, but in another it was really good fun.

Katie's mum and dad came over to hear them play, too, and I could tell they were really impressed. I don't think they recognised Matt – well, they hadn't seen him for years – and Mum and I didn't let on. We reckoned that the fewer people who knew Matt was in town, the better. They were a bit surprised to see Mum there, but she made some feeble excuse about me wanting to hire the band for a party in the summer so she'd come to hear them.

They were all a bit rusty at first. They'd not played together for weeks, so it took a while to get everything right. And to begin with, Matt was very jumpy. But as soon as they all got into the music, they seemed to forget about Keith and his heavies and relax and enjoy themselves.

I was so proud of Matt. I know this is what he should be doing. He's just so good at it. Music's in his blood. It's so unfair that things have been so difficult for him – for all of them. Life's been stacked against him – and it's all been because of bloody Keith.

The party went really well, although I couldn't relax and enjoy it myself. Every time the door opened, I was terrified that Keith would walk in and ruin everything. So a lot of the time I just hung around chatting to friends, one eye on the band, another on the door.

I didn't see the music guy from London come in. He must have slipped in really quietly and just merged into the crowd. But I was suddenly aware of this man standing at the back of the hall, listening.

I was sure it was him. It had to be.

I didn't know whether I should go up and talk to him or if I should just let him listen. Matt and the others hadn't noticed him either and I was glad. Matt was being himself, funny and relaxed, and the band were playing some great stuff, and playing it really well.

Most of the lyrics had been written by Matt and they came from the heart. He'd been there, in despair, separated from his family, with no self-esteem. Those songs were written with passion, and it showed. The words and the music meshed together so well, too. I can't really describe it.

In the end, I went up to the guy when one set had just finished.

'Hi,' I said. 'I'm Matt's sister. Matt who runs the band,' I added.

He smiled and nodded. I didn't know what to say. I didn't want to blow it for Matt by jumping in and praising him to the skies.

'Shall I tell him you're here?'

The guy shook his head. 'No,' he said slowly. 'I'll listen to the next set first.'

Well, at least he was going to give the band a fair hearing.

I went and fetched him a drink, then I sort of shuffled away, but I kept my eye on him from a distance.

Then a crowd of my friends surrounded me and I lost sight of him. The next time I looked for him, he'd gone.

I panicked then, thinking he'd lost interest, but then I spotted him at the edge of the stage. The band had just stopped playing and he was talking to them. Matt and his friends were listening intently. I crossed my fingers and prayed.

Well, it must have worked! Soon after that he left. I rushed over to Matt, but they'd started playing again, so I had to shut up until they'd finished. But I watched them carefully and every now and then, they'd glance at each other and grin.

At last I found out.

'He liked us,' said Matt. 'He really liked us!'

'So, what's going to happen?'

'He wants us to do a recording session in his studio next week and make a professional demo tape so he can see how we sound with all the high tech stuff to back us up.'

'Matt, that's FANTASTIC!'

'Nothing's settled, Becky. It's only a demo tape.' But he couldn't keep the excitement out of his voice.

'Are you going to be able to get all the gear to the studio?'

Matt nodded. 'Mum's lent us a bit of cash so we can hire taxis.'

'What about Keith? You didn't let on to the guy about Keith?'

Matt frowned. 'No. We'll have to be careful, Becky. Keith's bound to find out that we've been playing here; he's going to try and find us. He'll try even harder now.'

'You're going back to London tonight, aren't you?'

'Yeah. We reckoned we should get out of Bedford right away, before the news breaks and he finds us here.' He grinned. 'Some woman in a wig's going to drive us back.'

Poor Mum! She'll be shattered. But it's the best thing to do.

So, here I am, in the early hours of the morning, waiting for Mum to get home. She's made some elaborate plan to get home on the early train and pick up her car from Tesco's. Then, I guess, she'll need to sleep for a week!

Melbourne, October 1867

After Amos and Flo had left, the hotel was peaceful and calm for a while. The morning routines started up, rooms were cleaned, food prepared and bookings taken.

Nothing was amiss. Everyone knew that Amos had left for a holiday in Sydney.

It was not until nearly noon that the peace was shattered.

Francis Delaware came striding into the lobby and banged his fist on the desk. Harriet jumped back, nervously.

'Where the hell is that young cur?' he shouted.

'I'm sorry, sir,' said Harriet. 'I don't understand.'

Henry heard the commotion and he came out from the office behind the desk. 'Can I help you, sir?' he asked politely, though, inwardly he was very nervous when he saw who it was. What had Amos done?

Francis Delaware was very red in the face. 'Where's that bastard son of yours?' he demanded of Henry.

Henry swallowed, trying his best to keep calm. 'Amos is away,' he said evenly.

'Where's he gone, man? Where's he taken my daughter?'

Henry lost all his composure then. 'What?' he stuttered. 'What did you say?'

Francis Delaware leant forward, pushing Harriet aside and taking the lapels of Henry's jacket roughly in his hands.

'Don't play the innocent with me, man!' he shouted, shaking Henry. 'My daughter's disappeared and she's run off with that damn son of yours!'

All Henry's instincts were to hit Francis Delaware, but with iron self control he removed the man's hands from his jacket and stepped back.

'I assure you, sir,' he said quietly. 'I know nothing of this. Amos has gone to Sydney to visit a friend.'

'Bah! Sydney! A friend! I tell you man, he's eloped with my daughter and, by God, when I find him I'll make him wish he'd never been born!'

Henry was very white and, to his irritation, he could feel his hands tremble, but he stood his ground.

'They love each other, Mr Delaware. If what you say is true; if Amos really has taken Florence away, then I'm sure he will have done the honourable thing; he will have wed her.'

Francis Delaware was purple with rage. 'What honour is there in doing it behind my back? He knows I expressly forbade it!'

Henry said nothing.

Francis Delaware continued. '*Where* in Sydney?' he shouted. 'Did he leave no address?'

'At the home of a friend from London. That's all I know.'

'I shall find them. I shall find them and take Florence back to her home. Back where she belongs!'

Henry stayed silent.

Francis Delaware turned then and almost ran towards the main doors, colliding with a porter carrying bags. He didn't apologise, but just looked back at Henry.

'My God, man! I'll get you for this,' he yelled. 'I'll make sure no people of quality ever darken the doors of this hotel again.'

As soon as he was through the doors and out of sight, Henry sank down in the nearest chair and put his head in his hands.

'Oh Amos! Amos!' he muttered.

He was so full of his own thoughts that it was a while before he raised his head and saw that Harriet was still standing, rigid as a statue, behind the desk. He got up and went over to her.

'Oh Harriet, if this is true, if Amos and his Flo have run away, I dread what will 'appen. It will bring such trouble on us all.'

He stretched out his hand to stroke her hair, but she flinched away from him.

'Don't touch me!' she shouted.

'Harriet!'

'The lying *bastard*,' she screamed. 'How *dare* he deceive us! How *dare* he go off with that overbred strumpet!'

'Hush, Harriet,' said Henry. 'We don't know if it's true!'

'Of course it's true! He gave in too readily, don't you see? He knew he couldn't get her father's consent so they laid their plans secretly, the scheming wretches.'

Henry was puzzled by the violence of her words. 'But Harriet,' he said gently. 'They *do* love each other. You could see that.'

'Love!' she screamed. 'What does he know of love?'

Then, without any warning, she picked up a heavy vase of flowers from the desk and flung it on the floor. Henry looked on as the vase broke into fragments, the flowers scattered and a pool of water spread across the marble tiles.

He was too surprised to say anything and, in any event, Harriet gave him little chance, for she immediately gathered up her skirts and ran, sobbing, up the stairs to their quarters on the next floor.

At the top of the stairs, she stopped and turned, screaming hysterically to anyone who would listen: 'I HATE him!'

Then Molly appeared. She had run from their quarters to the top of the stairs when she heard Harriet's screams.

'Harriet, love, whatever is the matter?'

She went to comfort her, but Harriet pushed her away.

'I HATE him,' she screamed again. 'I hate you all! It will never be the same again.'

Bedford, present day, April

Matt's just rung me! It's happening. It's really happening!

The band are being given a contract. It's not big bucks or anything, but it's with a proper record company. It's a beginning.

And the really great thing is that Matt has told them all about Keith's company and the money they owe on the equipment. And the record company have got their legal people on to it and they are going to pay Keith off! They've worked out a deal so Matt and the others can pay them back, gradually, over the months, taking it out of what the band earns.

The relief in Matt's voice! I don't think he can believe it.

I told him to be careful; not to sign a thing until he's talked it over with Mum. But they must think a lot of Jacob's Footstool if they're prepared to do that sort of deal.

It's BRILLIANT!

I can't wait to tell Mum. She'll be over the moon.

Melbourne, June 1868

It had been a terrible few months. Francis Delaware had done everything he could to get Flo back, but he had reckoned without Amos. He tried to get the marriage annulled, but Amos had made sure everything was legal. Sometimes Amos would see one of the Delaware lackeys loitering in the street outside, but he made sure that Flo never left the hotel on her own.

Amos had friends too, and they rallied round. To be sure, most of the Delaware cronies boycotted the hotel, but there were plenty of other people who came. Some of them, it must be said, to catch sight of the couple who had flouted the great Francis Delaware and caused such a scandal in Melbourne, but these gawpers often came back again because of the comfort of the place and its relaxed atmosphere and good food.

To begin with Flo was very nervous, jumping at the slightest sound, startled by shadows. She had good reason to be afraid; her father had sworn to bring her home and he was not a man to be thwarted. Once or twice she managed to meet her mother secretly. She knew how difficult things were for her, but as Flo pointed out – gently but firmly – she was over twenty-one and her loyalty was to her husband. And there was no doubting her commitment – to Amos, to Henry and Molly and to the hotel.

With her natural good taste, she gradually brought in a few changes, too, though she had to be careful not to offend Harriet.

But Harriet would have been offended whatever she did. She would never meet Flo's eyes, she answered her in monosyllables, and she seldom smiled. Amos had to take her off the front desk and give her other duties behind the scenes because she was so sullen with the guests. Now it was usually Flo who greeted them and made them feel welcome.

So they had struggled on. At first, Henry was angry with Amos. 'Couldn't you 'ave waited, son? Until the hotel was more established?'

Amos grinned. 'There would 'ave bin a scandal whenever we did it,' he said. 'And you've got to admit it's brought in a good few punters to see the man chosen by the great Francis Delaware's daughter, in the teeth of 'is opposition.'

'Aye. I'll grant you that, son,' said Henry, smiling. 'And she's a worker, your Flo. No fancy airs and graces, and she gets on with things.'

Amos glowed with pleasure. 'See, father, I told you she'd fit in 'ere. She'll add a bit of class to the place, too!'

Henry shrugged. 'Class,' he mused. 'We never 'ad much of that back in London, son!'

'Don't look back, father,' said Amos, gently. 'Mam and the others have made a success of themselves, too. They've changed and all.'

'It couldn't 'ave 'appened there, though,' said Henry. 'You marrying the likes of Flo.'

Amos shook his head. 'No, it couldn't 'ave 'appened there.'

Henry changed the subject. 'I'm worried about Harriet,' he said suddenly.

Amos nodded. 'She's gone right back to being that moody girl I got so riled by up in Gippsland,' he said.

'What ails 'er?' asked Henry. 'D'you know?'

Amos looked down at the floor. 'She's jealous, father.'

'Of you?'

'Of me, of 'ow she 'as to share you and Molly now. And of Flo, and of the love we have for each other.'

'But she should be 'appy for that,' said Henry, frowning.

Amos shrugged. 'Jealousy's in 'er nature,' he said. 'There's naught we can do.'

Henry sighed. 'Mebbe she'll grow out of it,' he said.

'Mebbe.'

But she only seemed to get worse. As things improved in the hotel, the regular guests returning and its reputation growing, Harriet became more and more inward looking and angry.

And then, one night, everything came to a head.

It was a rare occasion when they were all sitting down to a meal together. Amos looked across at Flo and smiled. 'Shall we tell them now?'

She nodded and blushed slightly.

'Father, Molly, Harriet,' said Amos. 'Flo is expecting a child!'

Immediately, Molly ran to Flo and flung her arms around her, and Henry stood up and came over to Amos and slapped him on the back.

For a moment, no one noticed that Harriet had left the room, but when they did, Molly went after her.

It was a long time before Molly returned to the others, who were by now sitting happily round the table talking about the future.

'Is Harriet all right?' asked Amos.

Molly frowned. 'She won't be comforted,' she said anxiously, 'And I can't get her to say what ails 'er.'

'Leave 'er be, Molly,' said Henry.

'I don't like to leave 'er like this,' said Molly, 'But she wouldn't have me stay with 'er.'

Amos frowned. He probably understood Harriet better than any of them. He knew how powerful was her jealousy. And now there would be someone else to envy, someone else to get in the way of her parents' affections for her.

He sighed to himself. He was bursting with pride and happiness and he wished he could make Harriet share in that happiness.

Harriet never reappeared and, eventually, the rest of them did the evening chores without her and retired to bed.

It was Flo who woke first, coughing and spluttering. She shook Amos.

'Amos! Wake up! Quick! There's smoke everywhere!'

Amos woke up slowly, then he, too, started to choke.

'My God, Flo! The place is on fire!'

'Get to the others, Amos. Check that they're safe.'

'Not before you,' said Amos firmly.

He tried to get to the door, but he was driven back by smoke and flames. Then he threw open the window.

'I'll jump,' he said. 'Then I'll catch you.'

He jumped out of the window and landed awkwardly on the ground below, rubbing a twisted ankle.

'Now, jump!'

For a moment, Flo hesitated. 'The baby?' she whispered, but he didn't hear her.

'JUMP!'

And indeed, there was little choice. Flames and choking smoke were sweeping across their room. Without another backward glance, she jumped and Amos caught her in his arms. The impact unbalanced him and he staggered back and fell, but neither of them was badly hurt.

They ran round to the front of the hotel and raised the alarm. Flo wanted to go back inside, but Amos wouldn't let her.

'No Flo, please. Think of our baby.' Then, just pausing to snatch a heavy cloth from a table to put over his mouth and nose, he headed back up the stairs again.

People were running to and fro, and Amos shouted instructions as he raced along the landing, first to Harriet's room which was empty, then towards Molly and Henry's room. They were safe. They had heard the commotion and come out.

'The fire's worst in my room,' said Amos. 'It's not so bad in the rest of the rooms.'

'Where is Harriet?' screamed Molly.

'I've just checked her room,' he yelled back. 'The fire hasn't reached it.'

'Was she there?'

'No, she must have gone outside.'

'Oh, thank God,' said Henry.

Together, they got the guests safely outside and organised the staff with buckets of water. Once all the flames had been dowsed, Amos and Flo and Henry and Molly inspected the damage.

'It could be worse,' said Amos, wearily drawing his hand over his sweating, smoke stained brow.

Molly squeezed his hand. 'Aye,' she said quietly. 'We're all safe. That's what counts.'

'I'll go outside and fetch Harriet in,' said Henry.

But a few minutes later, he returned.

'They've not seen 'er,' he said. 'She's not bin outside.'

They looked at each other in horror.

'Where is she?' said Molly, 'Let me go and look upstairs again.'

Amos stopped her. 'No, Molly, I'll go. You stay here.'

He opened all the doors and looked into the smouldering rooms, but he couldn't see her anywhere. Perhaps, after all, she was outside.

Then he looked in his room, his and Flo's, although he was sure she couldn't be there. He was about to close the door when he noticed what he thought was a heap of bed linen lying in the corner. Then it moved slightly.

Feeling sick, he approached and looked down.

A little later, he emerged, the unconscious body in his arms.

At the top of the stairs, he looked down at the

frightened faces below. 'Fetch a doctor,' he said quietly. 'She's badly burned, but she's still alive.'

What he didn't tell them was why he had delayed for a few precious moments. He had stopped to prize the remaining matches from her hand and stuff them into the pocket of his breeches.

Bedford, present day, April

We've spent hours at the hospital, me and Matt, sitting by Mum's bed. It's been horrible. There were tubes and machines all round her.

We kept telling her that Matt's going to be all right, now. That he's out of trouble and that Keith can't hurt him any more.

But she can't hear us. Not a flicker. Nothing.

Somehow I just know Keith's behind it all. He's the reason why she's lying here. I'm sure he's responsible. He must be.

No one saw what happened. There was no other car involved. It seems that Mum suddenly swerved out of control and crashed into a wall.

That's not like Mum. She's such a careful driver.

I'm certain it was Keith. Was he following her? Scaring her? Could he have heard that Matt had been playing at Katie's party? Had that made him angry? So angry that he'd forced her off the road, scared her enough to lose control of the car?

The crash happened just after I'd heard from Matt.

I'd kept trying Mum on her mobile but there was only the answerphone.

So I decided to crash out in front of the telly and wait for her to come home. And that's when the police came to the house. There were two of them, a young woman and an older man and, immediately I saw them, I knew something dreadful had happened. It was strange, though. I was so sure it was Matt who was in trouble that it took me a moment or two to grasp what they were saying – that Mum had been in a car crash and that she was in intensive care in the hospital.

They were really kind and they waited while I phoned Matt (thank God he's got a mobile now; the record people insisted) then they drove me straight to the hospital.

I felt numb when I saw her. So still and pale with a huge bruise on her head. And all those wires and tubes!

Matt got there as soon as he could and we just sat either side of her, holding a hand each.

We kept talking to her – the nurse said it was important – and telling her how we needed her.

Several times I lost it completely and sobbed. 'Mum, please don't die. Please wake up. PLEASE!'

Matt tried to keep it together, but he wasn't that successful, either.

As the hours dragged on through the night, we talked to each other too. Both of us are certain that Keith was involved, but there's no way of proving it.

'He's dangerous, Becky,' said Matt. 'And jealous. He's still obsessed with her. If he can't have her, somehow he's going to make sure no one else does.'

'How can anyone be so twisted?'

Matt shrugged. 'He's mental, Beck. I mean seriously mental.' Then he sighed. 'I wish we could prove he'd been stalking her. Then maybe the police would check on his movements and see if he was in the area when the crash happened.'

I'd nodded. But we hadn't got any proof, so what could we do? We'd told the police about Keith, but they'd said there was no evidence of any other vehicle being involved.

But he didn't have to be in a car, for goodness sake! He could scare her just as much in other ways, couldn't he?

The nurse said we could stay in the hospital for the night and showed us where we could sleep, but even though I was shattered I couldn't settle. I tossed and turned, then I started writing this on some scraps of paper I found in the bin.

And suddenly, as I was rummaging in the rubbish, I remembered something.

I still had it! I still had that scrap of paper Katie and I had saved from the bin bags. The threatening note from Keith. It had his signature on it – he'd not bothered to disguise who it was from.

And another thing. Mum had talked to her lawyer friend about Keith stalking her. So someone else knew about him and what he was doing to us.

So there was proof – of a sort.

It was a start, anyway. A tiny ray of hope.

We can't go on like this, with Keith's shadow looming over us all the time, specially with Mum like she is.

The next morning

Gran and Grandad arrived at the hospital this morning. They stayed for an hour or so, then they took Matt and me back to the house.

It seems so strange to be here without Mum. Gran and Grandad say they'll stay for as long as they're needed. And Matt's going to stay for a couple of days, too, but he's got to get on with his life. He's got to get back to London – especially now, now he's got so much going for him. It would really please Keith if Matt lost it now, crumpled up because of Mum. For Mum's sake, for mine, and for his too, he's got to make something of Jacob's Footstool. He's got to make it work.

While Gran was fussing about in the kitchen, making us a huge lunch which I knew I wouldn't be able to eat, I suddenly remembered that I'd wanted to ask her something. For ages, I'd been meaning to ask her where the snuffbox and gold watch came from.

But it's not important now.

Melbourne, July 1868

It was a month after the fire. Harriet had been badly burned about the face and hands and she'd breathed in a lot of smoke, but she had survived. She lay upstairs, in one of the undamaged rooms, swathed in bandages. A doctor came most days and Henry and Molly were at her bedside day and night.

Flo had lost her baby and, for the first time since they'd met, Amos saw defeat in her eyes.

It was almost more than he could bear, but he forced himself to work non-stop, to get the hotel operating again. All the staff supported him. They did jobs they'd never done before – painting and scrubbing, nailing and hammering. And, in truth, the damage looked worse than it was. Three of the bedrooms were unusable and a lot of curtains and carpets had been ruined, but the structure was still sound.

'It'll not be long, Flo,' promised Amos.

Flo smiled wanly. She was still very weak from the miscarriage. She looked about her at the mess and sighed.

Amos came over to her and pressed her hand. 'We'll do it. Together we'll get it to rights, I promise.'

Flo raised herself from her lethargy and made a big effort to smile properly. 'Of course we will,' she said.

But the spark that Amos loved so dearly had left her eyes and he yearned to see it return.

Henry tried to help Amos. He supervised the

repainting of all the woodwork – but with little enthusiasm. He had aged ten years in the last month. He couldn't bear to see his beautiful Harriet scarred and ugly and hardly responding as she lay listlessly in her bed.

The stuffing had gone out of him and it was only Amos's determination that kept him going. 'We must get it back to normal, father, as quickly as possible,' Amos urged. And Henry nodded and smiled, but his heart was no longer in it. His heart was with his daughter and with his poor, distraught wife.

Sometimes Amos felt that he was bearing all their grief on his shoulders and all the responsibility for keeping them going: Flo, Molly, Henry and Harriet.

He tried not to think of the day of the fire when he'd found Harriet – clutching the matches. He tried not to blame her when it was she, after all, who had suffered the worst of them all.

But it was hard.

He didn't think things could get any worse. He was sure that they would weather the storm, get over this and go forward.

But another shock was to come; the worst shock of all.

The secret he'd guarded so carefully and kept from Flo – from them all – came out.

One day a small, scruffy man came into the front of the hotel. He was shabbily dressed and had ingrained dirt in the creases in his face and under his fingernails. He was holding a young child in his arms.

Flo was at the desk. She looked up and quickly took in his dress and manner; probably a miner, she thought. She smiled at the child but it cringed back into the man's chest.

'Yes?' she asked.

'I've come to see Amos Harris.' said the man.

'I'm sorry, I'm afraid he's busy,' said Flo. 'Can I help?'

The man coughed and Flo realised that he was extremely ill. The wheezing and spluttering went on and on. When at last he could draw breath, he said, 'It's private.'

Flo frowned. Something about the man made her nervous, though she couldn't say what.

'Very well,' she said at last. 'Wait here.'

She fetched Amos, who came reluctantly.

'He said he must see you,' said Flo. 'He won't tell me what he wants.'

Amos was still grumbling when he came into the hotel lobby, but as soon as he saw the man and the child, he stopped abruptly. Flo looked on, puzzled, as he clenched his fists by his side.

'What are you doing here?' he said very quietly to the man.

The man looked him full in the face. 'I can't care for him any longer,' he said, indicating the child in his arms.

'But you have money. I made sure you had money!'

The man never stopped looking at Amos. 'It isn't the money,' he said slowly. 'It's my health, Amos. His mother died giving birth to him and now I'm dying, too. You'll have to care for your son yourself.'

And with that, he set the little boy down, gave him a quick pat on the head and limped towards the door. Just before he left, he turned and looked at Flo.

'You'll see to it he's cared for, won't you, ma'am?' Then when she didn't answer, he went on. 'He goes by the name of William.' He hesitated. 'It was my daughter's wish to call him that.'

As his grandfather went out of the hotel, the little boy instantly started screaming and started to stagger after him.

For a moment, Amos and Flo stared at each other, then Flo ran to the child and gathered him in her arms.

As she comforted him, she looked again at Amos and tears were running down her cheeks.

'I'm sorry,' said Amos. 'I'm so sorry.' He started to come over to her but she backed away, burying her head in the child's filthy neck.

'What else, Amos?' she whispered. 'What else do I have to bear?'

But her words were drowned by William's yells . . .